DON'T DO IT.

Fargo hadn't intended to knock Deputy Sheriff Harney Roscoe through the wall of the Hog's Breath saloon. It just happened to be a thin wall and a solid haymaker.

Wood cracked, splinters flew and Roscoe did a backward Virginia reel, stumbling across the boardwalk and landing flat on his back in the wagon-rutted main street of Busted Flush, Arkansas.

Fargo stepped through the newly created exit just as Roscoe, his pasty face swollen and bleeding, slapped at his holster.

Fargo's walnut-gripped Colt formed a blur from holster to hand.

"If you even *sneeze*," Fargo warned in a deceptively soft tone, "you'll never hear the *gesundheit*."

THE TRAILSMAN

#390

DEVIL'S DEN

by

Jon Sharpe

A SIGNET BOOK

SIGNET
Published by the Penguin Group
Penguin Group (USA) LLC, 375 Hudson Street,
New York, New York 10014

USA | Canada | UK | Ireland | Australia | New Zealand | India | South Africa | China
penguin.com
A Penguin Random House Company

First published by Signet, an imprint of New American Library,
a division of Penguin Group (USA) LLC

First Printing, April 2014

The first chapter of this book previously appeared in *Outlaw Trackdown*, the three
hundred eighty-ninth volume in this series.

 REGISTERED TRADEMARK—MARCA REGISTRADA

ISBN 978-0-451-46794-2

Printed in the United States of America
10 9 8 7 6 5 4 3 2 1

The Trailsman

Beginnings . . . they bend the tree and they mark the man. Skye Fargo was born when he was eighteen. Terror was his midwife, vengeance his first cry. Killing spawned Skye Fargo, ruthless, cold-blooded murder. Out of the acrid smoke of gunpowder still hanging in the air, he rose, cried out a promise never forgotten.

The Trailsman they began to call him all across the West: searcher, scout, hunter, the man who could see where others only looked, his skills for hire but not his soul, the man who lived each day to the fullest, yet trailed each tomorrow. Skye Fargo, the Trailsman, the seeker who could take the wildness of a land and the wanting of a woman and make them his own.

Devil's Den, Northwest Arkansas, 1860—where Fargo locks horns with a pack of savage killers in a deadly corner of Ozark country.

1

Fargo hadn't intended to knock Deputy Sheriff Harney Roscoe through the wall of the Hog's Breath saloon. It just happened to be a thin wall and a solid haymaker.

Wood cracked, splinters flew and Roscoe did a backward Virginia reel, stumbling across the boardwalk and landing flat on his back in the wagon-rutted main street of Busted Flush, Arkansas.

Fargo stepped through the newly created exit just as Roscoe, his pasty face swollen and bleeding, slapped at his holster.

Fargo's walnut-gripped Colt formed a blur from holster to hand.

"If you even *sneeze*," Fargo warned in a deceptively soft tone, "you'll never hear the *gesundheit*."

A menacing, metallic click sounded on Fargo's left.

"All right, Skye," said an amiable voice, "toss that lead chucker down."

Fargo did as ordered and glanced to his left. Sheriff Dub Gillycuddy, a big Colt's Dragoon filling his hand, stood grinning at him.

"Trailsman," he said, leathering the big gun, "most jaspers are content to just raise hell—you always have to *tilt* it a few inches. All right, what's the larceny this time?"

"Hell, I didn't start it, Dub. I was in a friendly game of pasteboards when Roscoe here horned in and declared table stakes. When I told him it was strictly a two-dollar limit, he took exception."

"Uh-huh. And who tossed the first punch?"

"Well," Fargo admitted, "that would be me. But only after Deputy Roscoe tried to jerk me outta my chair."

The sheriff glanced at his vanquished deputy. "Is that the straight, Harney?"

But just then Roscoe made a sucking noise like a plugged drain and passed out.

Sheriff Gillycuddy studied his badly mauled deputy for a few moments, noting the split and swelling lips, bloodied nose and blue-black left eye already puffing up like a hot biscuit.

"Hell's fire, Fargo! If you'd beat on him any longer, I'd have to pick him up with a blotter."

"The son of a bitch bit me, Dub. I can't abide that in a sporting fight, not from a man."

A portly, balding man in a filthy apron stepped through the hole in the wall. "Sheriff, *look* at what Fargo done to my place!"

"Actually," Fargo pointed out, "it was Roscoe who went through the wall."

"At the end of *your* fist! Somebody owes me—"

Gillycuddy raised a hand to silence the sputtering barkeep. The sheriff was a handsome, avuncular man in his early fifties whose easygoing manner and broad-minded tolerance kept getting him elected although the law-and-order faction wondered how his monthly rent could be twice his salary.

"Just hold your horses, Silas. Who started this catarumpus?"

"I can't rightly say. But Fargo seemed peaceful enough before Harney showed up."

The sheriff cast another glance toward his supine deputy. "Hell, there ain't nothing but bone twixt his jug handles and he's always on the scrap. I'll 'low as how it wasn't likely you, Skye, who started the dustup. But I couldn't just let you shoot my deputy. He's also the town dogcatcher and hog reeve."

"But my wall!" Silas protested. "That hole—"

"The town fund will pay for it," Gillycuddy cut him off. "Skye, I'm gonna have to toss you in the pokey for one night. And there'll be a five-dollar fine for disturbing the peace. Here, lend a hand . . ."

Fargo and the sheriff dragged Roscoe up onto the relative safety of the boardwalk. As the two men crossed the wide street toward the jailhouse, Fargo spoke up.

"Dub, I don't mind a night in the calaboose. But as to that five-dollar fine . . . there's a reason I was playing a limit game."

"Light in the pockets, huh? Sorry, old son. If you can't post the pony, it's a dollar a day in jail."

Fargo shrugged. The tall, broad-shouldered, slim-hipped frontiersman was clad in fringed buckskins and wore a dusty white hat with a bullet hole in the crown. A close-cropped beard and lake blue eyes set off his weather-bronzed face.

"Is the food any better," he asked, "since last time you jugged me?"

"The eats are tolerable if you pick the weevils out. But I only got the one cell, and I'm 'fraid you're gonna have to share it with the most foul-tempered Injin I ever met up with."

"What tribe?"

"Ahh, I b'lieve he's a half-breed Choctaw. That red son smells like a bear's cave."

"Jumped the rez?" Fargo meant the sprawling Indian Territory, which began only about ten miles west of this rugged corner of the Ozark region.

"I s'pose, but his English is mighty good—or at least his cussin' is. I'm about to shoot that hot-jawing son of a buck. Won't give me his name, but he don't hesitate to give me the rough side of his tongue."

The sheriff suddenly laughed. "Why, that blanket ass is plumb loco. His damn saddlebags was stuffed with tossed-out envelopes he took when the post office took out their trash. Won't tell me why."

Fargo's growing nubbin of suspicion hardened into a certainty. "Now this Choctaw . . . is he heavyset with a string of bright-painted magic pebbles around his neck?"

Gillycuddy's head snapped toward Fargo. "You know him?"

"He goes by the name of Cranky Man. He saved my life once a few miles from here near Lead Hill."

"Cranky Man, huh? Well, mister, he is that. I mighta guessed you'd be chummy with a reprobate like him. The hell's he want with all them envelopes?"

"He can't read, so he thinks there's big magic in white man's handwriting. First time I ever saw him he was stealing old army contracts from one of my saddle pockets."

"Yeah? Well, that Indian wasn't born—he was squeezed

out of a bar rag. When I arrested him he was drunker'n the lords of Creation. All he's done since, when he ain't cussin' me out, is demand liquor. Claims his religion requires him to drink."

Gillycuddy pulled up in front of the jailhouse door. "Le'me have that toothpick in your boot. And where's your Henry?"

"Locked up at Drake's livery," Fargo replied, reluctantly surrendering his Arkansas toothpick. "I want a chit for these weapons."

The sheriff grunted and led the way into a cubbyhole office with wanted dodgers plastered to the walls and a battered kneehole desk. Fargo immediately spotted Cranky Man in the cramped cell, sitting on one of two army cots and picking his teeth with a match. He saw Fargo and did a double take.

"Skye Fargo! Hell, I figured you were pegged out by now."

"Sorry to disappoint you. Last time I saw you, you said you were headed back to Mississippi."

"I say a lot of things I don't do." Cranky Man aimed a malevolent glance at the sheriff. "Won't matter now. If these peckerwoods have their way, I'm gonna be the guest of honor at a hemp social."

Gillycuddy stuffed Fargo's knife and gun in a drawer and banged it shut. "That's a lie on stilts, savage. I'm holding you until a tumbleweed wagon rolls through town and hauls your worthless, flea-bit ass back to the Nations, where Andy Jackson, in his infinite wisdom, sent you."

"Fuck him and fuck you, starman," the Choctaw shot back. "You and your whole cockeyed town can kiss my red ass."

Fargo bit back a grin as he watched the sheriff's normally mellow features suffuse with purple anger.

"You just keep pushing me, chief. You couldn't lick snot off your upper lip, so don't be playing top dog around me."

"Who'd you kill?" Cranky Man asked Fargo when the sheriff admitted him into the cell.

"A little misunderstanding with a deputy," Fargo replied, sitting on the empty cot.

The Choctaw had clearly fallen on hard times. Beggar's lice leaped from his clothing, and the weathered grooves of his face had deepened. His beaded moccasins were frayed and torn, and some of the beadwork was missing from his deerskin shirt.

"Got any Indian burner?" Cranky Man asked hopefully.

"Nope."

Cranky Man swore. "What I wouldn't give right now to be a fish in an ocean of whiskey."

A buckboard rattled to a stop outside and Sheriff Gillycuddy glanced out the window. If a voice could frown, his did now. "Stand by for a blast. Here comes Marcella and Malinda Scott."

Fargo perked up at the mention of females. "Sisters or mother and daughter?"

"Sisters, and they're both lookers. They moved here from someplace in Ohio to take over the Ozark West Transfer Line. This was after old Tubby Scott, their uncle, turned up dead. He left the business to them, but all they've done is bollix it up but good. It ain't no job for calicos."

"Tubby Scott," Fargo repeated. "Yeah, I recall hearing about him—Orrin Scott. Made his pile hauling mail and freight between Fayetteville and Van Buren."

The sheriff nodded. "Until he was found dead one morning in the crapper behind the station house. His neck was snapped so hard, his head flopped around like it was attached to a rubber tether."

The door swung open to admit the prettiest whirling dervish Fargo had seen in some time. She flounced toward Gillycuddy's desk in a froufrou of rustling skirts.

"Sheriff," she demanded, "*what* are you going to do about Anslowe Deacon?"

Gillycuddy raised both hands like a priest blessing his flock. "Sheathe your horns, lady. You're pretty as a speckled pony, Miss Marcella, but you always rare up like a she-grizz with cubs."

Fargo sized up Marcella Scott with appreciative eyes. She had a startlingly pretty oval face with a high-bridged nose and green eyes blazing with indignation. Strawberry blond hair framed her face in a mass of ringlets.

"How pretty I am is nothing to the matter! If I were a man you'd take me more seriously!"

The sheriff shrugged indifferently. "No need to be so

snippety. It ain't my fault if Deacon runs a better short line than you do. That's competition for you."

"Competition? The man is a murdering criminal!"

The door opened again and a second breathtaking beauty—Malinda Scott, Fargo assumed—glided in much more demurely. She was shapely and petite with sun-streaked auburn hair barely controlled by tortoiseshell combs. Her lacquered straw hat featured a brightly dyed ostrich feather and gay "follow me lads" ribbons.

"Well, now, as to *criminals*," the sheriff told Marcella, "you're the one who's out of jail on bail, not Deacon. And bail can be revoked easy in Fayetteville."

"I did *not* steal Truella Brubaker's bracelet! I told you it was among the items taken from a locked desk in the station office—yet another crime you've done nothing about."

Malinda, who hadn't spoken a word yet, spotted Fargo and gave him a wide smile that threatened to crack her rosy cheeks.

"Yeah, well, I told you that's Fayetteville jurisdiction. And about them stolen items—there was something else besides that bracelet that you're agitated as all get-out about, Miss Marcella. Why'n't you put your cards on the table? I will help you, but I have to know what I'm looking for."

Fargo watched the imperious beauty blush. "Never mind that. Anslowe Deacon is a vicious criminal and you know it! You just lack the will and courage to do anything about it."

Gillycuddy let out a weary sigh and caught Fargo's eye. "You know, Trailsman, like they say—a pretty girl is a malady."

For the first time Marcella noticed Fargo with frowning disapproval. "The Trailsman? I've heard my workers mention that name. Are you Skye Fargo?"

"I am in this case," Fargo assured her, doffing his hat.

"And a criminal, I see."

"Oh, he's more or less law-abiding until he goes off on a bust," the sheriff vouchsafed. "I've never locked him up for anything worse than brawling. And once for—ahh—violating the Sunday blue laws."

"What you mean is that he fornicated on the Sabbath?"

"I wasn't Bible raised," Fargo offered in his own defense.

"Look at it this way, lady," Cranky Man piped up. "Every

time you whiteskins break one of them Ten Commandments of yours, you still got nine left."

"Yes, well, I'm sure you two ruffians manage to break all ten in one day."

"Usually by noon," Fargo assured her.

Marcella studied Fargo in silence for perhaps ten seconds. "Well, right now I *need* a ruffian. Are you interested in a job?"

"Oh, let's *do* hire him, sis," Malinda spoke up in a lilting, musical voice she must have worked on. "He's the most handsome, rugged man I've ever seen."

"You'll have to forgive my sister, Fargo," Marcella said, anger spiking her voice. "I won't call her a painted cat, but only because she doesn't charge money."

"Do tell?" Fargo said, raking his eyes over the comely lass.

"If I was paid what I'm worth," Malinda put in to spite her sister, "I'd be richer than the Vanderbilts."

"Well, now," Fargo said, "what a delightful girl."

Cranky Man snorted and Marcella slapped her sister. Malinda smiled at Fargo.

"Fargo, you best con this over good," the sheriff warned. "There's considerable stink brewing around here, all right, and it ain't all blowing off that Choctaw. I know how you are about women, but these two pert skirts will get you killed."

The acid-tongued Marcella whirled on the lawman. "Nobody asked you! If you'd do your job I wouldn't need to hire someone."

"I'll take the job," Fargo told her, "whatever it is. But only if you hire on Cranky Man here, too. He's not as worthless as he looks."

"I'm desperate," Marcella admitted.

"How 'bout it, Dub?" Fargo asked the sheriff. "Will you spring us?"

Gillycuddy pushed to his feet and snatched the cell key from a wall peg. "This time you get the breaks, Fargo. I'll even drop the fine. These gals could use your help, all right. 'Sides, I'm glad to get shut of this stinking savage. But *don't* go killing every living thing you see. I can only ignore so much, and if the hotheads around here get too riled up, all three of us could end up doing a dance on nothing."

7

He clanged the door open, then looked at Marcella. "Why are you ladies here, anyhow? Just to aggravate my ulcers?"

Marcella's pretty face turned grim. "I saved that for last. Please come outside."

All three men trooped out behind the women. Marcella pulled out the pin to drop the tailgate of the buckboard.

The sheriff's face turned fish-belly white. "Katy Christ!"

The dead man lying inside, glazed eyes staring wide open at nothing, was missing at least a fifth of his head.

2

When he was over his first jolt of shock, Sheriff Gillycuddy studied the dead man's blood-clotted face.

"I recognize that purple birthmark on his chin," he said. "It's Jimbo Miller."

"Yes," Marcella replied. "One of my best drivers murdered in cold blood. I thought you ought to see him before I take him to the undertaker. Just a little reminder of what happens when a duly sworn law officer shirks his duty."

The indignation in her tone reminded Fargo that this newly arrived outlander from Ohio didn't really yet understand her new home. The rugged and picturesque Ozark region was currently much more wide open and dangerous than many territories farther west favored by authors of the rapid-action whizbangs.

Missouri and Arkansas were two of the most violent places in America, home to criminal gangs—even small armies—that holed up in the remote, timber-girt hills and mountains, the countless caves, and struck with near impunity at travelers, then faded back to their outlaw camps. Gillycuddy could no more stem that violence than a broom could hold back the ocean.

"Miss Scott," Fargo said, "I'm sorry about your driver. But it's not fair to put this on the sheriff. He can't do anything unless there's reliable witnesses willing to come forward—witnesses who saw the shooter."

"Were there?" Gillycuddy asked.

"Of course not. But Anslowe Deacon is behind this, Sheriff, just as he was behind the murder of my uncle, and you know it. His Fort Smith Express Company is trying to wrest a lucrative Butterfield Stage Line mail contract away from

Ozark West Transfer, and his thugs have been harassing us mercilessly. If he can destroy our ability to keep schedule, that contract is his."

"I happen to believe at least some of that, Miss Marcella," Gillycuddy replied. "That's why I let Fargo out of jail to help you."

"This head shot," Fargo said, "looks to me like it might've been done with a Big Fifty Sharps. Those bullets packed to seven hundred grains can drop an elephant."

The sheriff nodded. "That shines. Unfortunately, even if it was, it's a popular rifle in these parts. Where'd it happen?"

"One of my other drivers, Sebastian Kilroy, found him just south of West Fork."

At this intelligence Fargo exchanged glances with the sheriff. West Fork was in the region known as Devil's Den, a rugged area of ravines, crevices and fracture caves in the Boston Mountains—a wild section of the Ozark country and criminal campground from time to time.

"What about the wagon?" Fargo asked.

"That's another clue. Neither the freight nor the mail was touched, although the two lead mules had been shot dead."

"So it wasn't a robbery," the sheriff mused aloud. "Just deliberate, stone-cold murder."

"Was there an express messenger along?" Fargo asked.

Marcella looked confused. "A what?"

"An armed guard with the driver."

"Oh. No, not for this run—we're short-handed."

"It likely wouldn't have mattered," Fargo opined. "An express guard is mostly useful if road agents get close in to grab the swag. A Big Fifty or a high-caliber rifle like it can score kills from eight hundred yards out."

Cranky Man elbowed Fargo's ribs. "You see him?"

Fargo nodded. In the waning light he had already noticed the stubbled profile of a man watching the group around the buckboard from across the street. The small, unblinking eyes of a lizard seemed fixated on Marcella especially—not that Fargo could call that unusual. The frontier was woman-starved and these two gals were a cut above.

But the rifle tucked under his arm was clearly a Big Fifty.

"That hombre glomming us from across the way," Fargo said, "anybody recognize him?"

"Eb Scofield," the sheriff replied. "Shiftless hill trash. That whole Scofield clan ain't worth the powder it would take to blow 'em to hell."

Scofield suddenly sauntered into the Hog's Breath.

"He watches me all the time," Marcella complained. "But then, plenty of uncouth men around here stare at both of us. Some of my workers think the Scofields work for Anslowe Deacon."

"I don't mind men staring at me," Malinda assured Fargo, sending him a come-thrill-me-knave smile.

"Get in the buckboard, you shameless hussy," Marcella snapped at her sister. She looked at Fargo, eyes carefully avoiding Cranky Man. "After we stop at the undertaker's we have a few errands to run. Do you know where the Ozark West home station is?"

Fargo nodded. "I've passed it a couple times since I rode in. Two miles due west of town on Old Granville Pike. Me and Cranky Man will pick up our horses and meet you there."

"I'll pay five dollars a day plus room and board," she said. "Do you agree to those terms?"

"Sounds jake to me," Fargo said. In fact, however, it wasn't enough for the kind of work in the offing—not for two men. But he couldn't blame her if she didn't believe Cranky Man was worth wages. He looked like a prime candidate for a glue factory.

"But I *won't* have Indians sleeping in the station house or eating at regular mealtimes. My workers won't stand for it."

Cranky Man flashed his trademark mirthless grin. "I won't poop in that crapper, neither. Sounds deadly."

She flushed to her earlobes.

"Bottle it," Fargo snapped at the Choctaw. "He'll be fine in the stock barn, Miss Scott, among his peers."

The sheriff snorted. "Marcella, this lice-ridden redskin is trouble on two sticks. Keep the whiskey locked up. A liquored-up Injin is one holy show."

By now the sun was setting in a blaze of gold glory behind the pine-forested mountains surrounding Busted Flush. The buckboard rattled off and Fargo and Cranky Man headed on foot toward Drake's livery at the east end of town.

"Know what I think?" Cranky Man said.

"If I say yes, will you shut up?"

Cranky Man invited Fargo to perform an anatomical impossibility upon himself. Then:

"Way I see it I ain't looking to die just so some high-toned white bitch can get rich. Hell, you seen that dead man—his skull looked like it was leaking cauliflower. I say we leave for a healthier climate. I know you're all het up to poke that pretty little slut Malinda. But, hell, you can get women anywhere you go."

"Look, we're both broke. Five dollars a day is no fortune once it's split two ways, but we'll get our eats tossed in. I can't blame you if you want to light a shuck, but I'm sticking."

"I do need money for whiskey and tobacco," Cranky Man conceded. "And long as I'm siding you we can use that story 'bout how I'm an Indian scout for the army—people tend to believe you, the fools. I'll do anything to stay off that damn reservation."

Fargo was no Indian lover, but he couldn't blame him. All five Civilized Tribes—Choctaws, Chickasaws, Cherokees, Creeks and Seminoles—had been forced out of their ancient homelands in the Southeast and into the Nations, the Indian Territory just west of Arkansas.

An 1830 treaty had granted the Choctaw nation "a tract of land west of the Mississippi." That tract, however, kept shifting and shrinking as white men found uses for the land.

"Yeah, I'm damned if I'd grub taters and answer roll calls," Fargo said. "When a man feels the tormentin' itch he likes to move on."

"What about that peckerwood who was spying on us?" Cranky Man changed the subject. "Eb Scofield. I figure you noticed his rifle."

"He just became one of our favorite boys," Fargo replied. "Matter fact, keep your eyes peeled for him now."

Both men stuck to the shadowy middle of the wide, washboard-rutted main street of Busted Flush, a jerkwater berg only a few miles south of Fayetteville. Oily yellow light spilled from windows and doorways, casting a foggy glow through which furtive, shadowy, sinister human forms flowed like aimless driftwood.

Bootheels raised a constant thump and shuffle along the raw-lumber boardwalks, punctuated by shouts, laughter, the ring of gold and silver coins on baize-topped tables. The metallic groan of hurdy-gurdies and the tinkle of player pianos added a note of desperate gaiety just waiting to be silenced by the inevitable authority of gunshots.

Fargo had seen and heard it hundreds of times before in countless flyblown settlements on the American frontier. Places like this were all right for an occasional carouse, but he was always glad to leave them behind for the solitude of a desert or the lonesomeness of the farthest corner of a canyon.

The two men swung into the hoof-packed yard of Drake's livery. Lester Drake, a hoary-headed elder with a face wrinkled like a peach pit, sat in front of a packing crate playing checkers against himself in the lamplight. Fargo scraped up just enough money to pay the stable charge for his Ovaro and Cranky Man's dish-faced skewbald.

Fargo's pinto stallion greeted the Trailsman by pushing his nose into Fargo's chest.

"Say, old roadster," Fargo called over to Drake as he slid the bridle over the Ovaro's ears and fastened the throat latch, "wha'd'ya know about the Scofield clan?"

"I know they're the most low-down and dangerous sons of bitches in this neck of the woods, most especial the five Scofield boys. There're three brothers sired by Rhodes Scofield and two cousins, both brothers, whelped by Lansford Scofield. Rhodes was et by his own hogs a few years back. Lansford died last year from straining too hard trying to take a shit. The man ate too damn much molasses."

Lester paused to watch Cranky Man tie the surcingle of his stuffed buffalo-hide saddle. He hawked up a wad of phlegm and spat it just inches from the Choctaw's feet. When Cranky Man failed to explode, Fargo guessed why and grinned.

"A-course," Lester resumed, "when it comes to the Scofield clan, there ain't a nickel's worth of difference twixt a brother and a cousin—if you take my drift?"

Fargo took his meaning, all right. In the backwoods of

Arkansas, a "virgin" was any girl who could run faster than her brothers.

"Say, Mr. Drake," Cranky Man spoke up in his best beggar-Indian wheedling tone, "any chance you could spare me and Fargo a snort?"

"John, you was lucky I even let a red heathen board his horse here. Specially a horse that ugly."

"Cranky Man's old man was a white soldier," Fargo put in truthfully, then tacked on a lie: "And this homely savage is working with me as an army scout."

"Well," Drake relented, retrieving a crockery jug from behind the crate, "I got paid a while back with some o' that panther piss they brew up in the hills. But go gradual, boys— I call it Bullfrog Gin: drink a little, hop a little and croak."

. He shook with laughter at his own joke and handed the jug to Fargo, who would have preferred a beer to cut the dust. He took a careful sip and immediately his eyes turned hot and filmed. It felt like a hot coal in his mouth and he spat it out without swallowing.

"Holy *shit*!" he gasped, handing the jug to Cranky Man. "That's liquid gunpowder. Take it easy."

Cranky Man ignored him, propping the jug on his shoulder and guzzling from it like it was water as Fargo and Drake stared, slack-jawed with amazement.

Cranky Man took the contents down by several inches, then belched and wiped his mouth with the back of his hand. He handed the jug back to Lester.

"It could use a bit more kick," the Choctaw opined. "I'd add a little more strychnine."

"Christ, he ain't a bit drunk!" Lester exclaimed.

"A man is never really drunk," Cranky Man informed him, "if he can lie on the floor without holding on."

"Let's rustle," Fargo said, swinging up into leather. "If that shit didn't kill you, I doubt if a bullet from a Big Fifty could do any damage."

3

A half hour's ride outside of Busted Flat, in a low, brushy hollow among densely forested mountains, a mud-daubed cabin sat in a small clearing dotted with tree stumps and strewn with animal bones. Three brothers who were part of the five men known locally as the Scofield boys had moved into it after the previous owner was found dead in a bear trap.

There were no coroner's courts in this stretch of the Ozark region, so nothing came of the rumors that the man caught by the right ankle in the trap also had a severely wrenched neck. But a few locals had noted that Tubby Scott, founder of the Ozark West Transfer Line, had died of exactly the same violent neck injury.

"Boys," Eb Scofield said, "it rocked me back on my heels when I seen Fargo chewin' the fat with them Scott sisters. They wasn't discussing the price of cheese, neither. I'm thinking Marcella was hiring buckskin boy. And from what I been hearing the last couple days, he ain't one for day labor."

Eb and his brothers, Romer and Stanton, sat around a crude deal table upon which sat an old skunk-oil lamp. Romer had recently stolen a side of bacon, and the three brothers were eating some of it out of the frying pan with clasp knives, washing it down with mountain lightning.

"I ain't frettin' it overmuch," declared Stanton, the oldest of the three and the brains of the Scofield outfit. He was skinny and knotty-muscled with a shrewd face and nervous manner that made others around him nervous too. "We know every holler and cave in this region, every old Indian trace and ambush nest. Fargo's a gone-up case."

Eb nodded. "We'll do for him, all right. But Deacon is

gonna shit strawberries into them fancy twilled britches of his when we tell him."

Stanton grinned, wiping his greasy mouth with his shirt-tail. "Ain't he, though? That sachet kitten won't even be able to get it up to screw his Cherokee whore."

Stanton swigged from the bottle and passed it over to Romer.

"That Cherokee is a nice little piece," Stanton resumed. "But hey! Both them Scott girls is prime woman flesh. I'd like to shove my hard pizzle 'bout a mile up their bellies. And, by God, all of us *will*."

At this talk Eb scowled darkly, his lizard eyes smoldering. "Women is *all* filthy harlots and I ain't never touching 'em. It's like Paw used to say: a woman's got seven holes in her body, and the devil can enter any of them—especially the belly mouth."

This prompted an explosion of laughter from Romer, a hairy brute with piglike eyes too small for his huge skull.

"Eb," he said, "you're a brain-addled motherfucker—you know that? That means the devil could slip in through a man's bunghole, too. We've seed how you go outta your way to stare at the older one, Marcella. You're wantin' to poke her so bad, you can't flush her outta your head."

Eb shook his head stubbornly. "She's a filthy, diseased harlot. I know somethin' 'bout her you two don't."

"You're alla time saying that," Stanton jeered. "But you're a shit-eatin' liar or you'd tell us."

"It's God's truth, Stanton."

"What? Is it somethin' you found when you stole the bracelet?"

"I ain't telling you nothing. But *I* know."

"Cow plop! But that's fine by me if you don't want a slice—leaves more pie for the rest of us. Cousin Bubba and Cousin Lem get a crack at both them gals, too."

"Bubba!" Romer hooted. "That half-wit can't even locate his own pee hole. Do you know that crazy bastard has took to carrying a pet rat in his pocket? He pets the damn thing and sings to it like it was a titty baby."

"He's ten bricks short of a load," Stanton agreed. "But he's strong as a grizz and he'll do any damn thing Lem tells him to. But listen here—I been thinkin' about Fargo. We can kill him sure as shit. But we need to do it quick 'fore he can deal himself deeper into this game. Deacon is mighty womanish, and if Fargo frights him off, us Scofield boys will lose our gravy."

"That's so. You got a plan?" Eb asked.

"Ain't I always? Look here . . . if the bitches has hired him on, he'll more'n likely stay at the main station house with them, right?"

Eb and Romer nodded. "He wouldn't pass up that pussy," Romer said.

"'At's right. That means sooner or later he'll have to use the shitter. To get to that big four-holer out behind the station, he'll have to cross about a hundred feet of wide-open flat. Eb, you can shoot the pecker off a wood tick with that Big Fifty. Tomorrow you'll get up before sunrise and pick you a nice, safe spot among the trees in all them hills that ring the station. Then you knock the son of a bitch out from under his conk cover."

"It'd be an easy shot," Eb agreed. "I popped Jimbo Miller over from five-hunnert yards. But what if Fargo ain't gotta take a crap?"

"Well, most men need to drain their snake every morning when they get up. And he ain't likely to piss into a cup, is he? There're women around—he can't just hang it out the window like Romer does."

"All right," Eb agreed. "Tomorrow morning I'll bore him through."

The Ozark West Transfer Line lay in a wide, shallow valley ringed by tall hills curtain-folding into mountains beyond them. The station house, a large one-story structure of sturdy pine logs, was the hub for several open-face stock sheds, a big hay barn, a pole corral and a smithy, all forming a circle around it.

Oak and dogwood trees shaded the house. Two Concord swift wagons and several Owensboro freight wagons with high sideboards were parked near the corral.

Fargo could see all of it under the generous illumination of a full moon and a clear, star-shot sky. He and Cranky Man had pulled rein just below the crown of a hill to avoid sky-lining themselves as they studied the layout.

"Looks peaceful enough," Fargo remarked. "But then, so does a graveyard."

"It won't be peaceful once you get there," Cranky Man countered. "Lead tends to fly around you."

"You saw Miller's corpse—lead's already flying."

Cranky Man twisted nervously around in the saddle, studying the trail behind them. "If that cracker Eb Scofield is in on this deal, that means his bunch already knows you've thrown in with the sisters."

"*We've* thrown in with the sisters," Fargo corrected him, grinning slyly in the moonlight. "C'mon—let's see how quick I can put you with your ancestors."

The two horsemen gigged their mounts up to a lope and closed the distance. They reined in well outside the station. Fargo was taking no chances in case sentries were posted.

"Hallo the station!" he called out. "Skye Fargo riding in with a friend!"

"Welcome, Trailsman!" a deep voice bellowed back. "I'm in the hay barn! Miss Scott said you'd be coming!"

The two men trotted their mounts up to the barn and lit down. They were greeted by an affable gent holding a kerosene lantern. He was of indeterminate middle age and wore thick bull-hide chaps.

"Howdy, Mr. Fargo," he said, glancing curiously at Cranky Man. "I'm Stan McKinney, the stock tender at this station. And this lad is Cecil. He's only twelve but he's tall for his age."

The kid hanging back shyly had an unruly shock of red hair and—even by lantern light—so many freckles he seemed to have no facial features.

"Pleased to meetcha, gents," Fargo said. "This ugly Indian is Cranky Man. But mind if we all get inside the barn? That lantern makes me a mite nervous."

"*Where* is my dang brain?" McKinney muttered, hustling back inside.

Huge stacks of fragrant hay occupied much of the barn, but a line of horse stalls had been built in the front.

"We use mules for pulling," McKinney explained as the

two men began to strip the rigs from their mounts. "They're in the stock sheds. Orrin Scott hired me on as a driver, but I had to give up on the whip—my hinges are stove up from my bronc-busting days in Kansas Territory."

He turned to the kid. "Cecil, pick two clean stalls and fork some hay into the nets. Rub these mounts down, too, and after you water them give 'em a few licks with the comb."

The kid, staring in apparent awe at Fargo, took the Ovaro's bridle reins reverently, as if he were taking possession of the Silver Chalice. McKinney chuckled. "Stir your stumps, mooncalf!"

He looked at Fargo and shrugged. "He don't mean to be rude by staring, Mr. Fargo. See, he reads all them penny press stories 'bout you and them others. He's a good kid. Mucks out the sheds and runs errands and such."

"Your son?"

"Nah, he's an orphan. One of our drivers, Sebastian Kilroy, brought him back here after his ma and pa was killed. This was during a raid on one of our coaches in the Devil's Den stretch. We don't hardly take no passengers these days, just mostly mail and freight."

"This raid," Fargo said, "was it Anslowe Deacon's work?"

"Nah. He's the thorn in our side now, but the attack that done for Cecil's ma and pa was pulled off by pukes out of Missouri. They ain't been around much lately since they been drawn into the Kansas troubles."

"Are you pretty sure," Fargo pressed, "that Deacon is the one behind the problems here?"

"Sure as sun in the morning. But he's a perfumed dandy and hires out the dirt work."

"To this bunch called the Scofield boys?"

"That's my hunch, but right now it can't be proved in court. It started 'bout three months back after Ozark West beat out Deacon's Fort Smith Express Company for a fat mail contract from Butterfield. Wasn't but a week later we found old Tubby—that's Orrin—murdered in the crapper. Mr. Fargo, I mean his head was damn near twisted off."

"No clues?"

"None. I think Sheriff Gillycuddy suspected right off that Deacon was behind it. But Deacon made sure he had him a perfect alibi: he was in St. Louis buying more freight wagons when it happened."

Fargo said, "Who do you think actually did the killing?"

"Well, according to Dame Rumor, that pus-gut prissy Deacon has got the Scofield boys on his payroll, and this murder had Bubba Scofield written all over it. He's stronger than horseradish and talk links him to other strangling deaths. Anyhow, for a time after that it was just stuff that a body might call accidental-like—rockslides across our routes and a washed-out bridge at the creek.

"Then it turned to sabotage of our conveyances and rock-salt ambushes on our teams that caused runaways and rollovers. Then, earlier today, the murder of Jimbo Miller—Miss Marcella told you about that."

Fargo nodded. "Look, I know Marcella is your boss. But tell me straight from the shoulder—does she know what she's doing?"

Stan glanced toward the open barn doors before answering in a lowered voice. "Well, them gals ain't been here too long, but neither one of 'em knows beans from buckshot about running a transfer line. Now, Malinda, the younger one, don't give a hoot in hell about learning the business. But Marcella, she's a quick study—*that* one's got starch in her petticoat."

"Yeah, she's a pip," Cranky Man muttered.

"What's that, Grouchy Man?"

"*Cranky* Man," the Choctaw corrected him.

"Sorry. Say, have you boys put on the nosebag yet?"

"I haven't had anything but a boiled egg all day," Fargo replied. "I wouldn't mind getting outside of some grub."

"I share the cooking with Malinda. When we head into the house I'll warm you boys up some biscuits and stew."

"Much obliged," Fargo said.

"How's chances for a snort?" Cranky Man asked hopefully, recognizing a friendly white man.

"I got a bottle of old orchard right here in the rag box," McKinney replied, pulling it out.

The three men passed the bottle around. Stan glanced over to make sure the kid was out of earshot. Then:

"Say, here's a lulu I heard yesterday from Sebastian. This

old maid goes to a doctor and complains how she's under the weather. The doc says, 'Was you ever bedridden?' 'Oh, yes,' she replies. 'And once in a sleigh.'"

Fargo chuckled and Cranky Man, who never offended a source of liquor, even slapped his thigh a few times.

"Well," McKinney said, "that's enough foolishness and it's getting late. You'll want to speak with the sisters. They turn in late, so they'll still be awake."

"I didn't notice a bunkhouse," Fargo said. "Do the hands sleep in the station house?"

"Yep. There ain't really enough to require a bunkhouse. We all turn in early 'cept for Dagobert. He's up till midnight most nights."

Fargo and Cranky Man exchanged amused glances.

"Dagobert?" Fargo repeated skeptically.

"Helluva moniker, ain't it? Dagobert Hastings . . . mostly we call him the Professor. He's the accountant and route supervisor. Old Tubby hired him on years ago. He's alla time talking up a dust cloud, and I'm hanged if I can follow most of it. But he knows this business inside out. Truth to tell, he's mostly the one running it while Marcella gets the hang of it."

Fargo stopped the other two men just inside the wide double doors. He had deliberately avoided looking into the lantern light so he wouldn't lose his night vision. He made a careful study of the moonlit landscape without.

"Besides the murder of Orrin Scott," Fargo said, "have you had any trouble right here at the station?"

"Nothing I know about," McKinney replied. "But I reckon we will now that you're here, Mr. Fargo—no offense intended."

"None taken, Stan. And you're right. We're gonna set up a night guard soon. The Scofield boys know I'm here, and they know why. They'll try to snuff my wick just like they did Orrin's. And they won't stop with me."

4

The large central room of the station house was comfortable and practical, with pine-board walls and a big fieldstone fireplace. Much of the furniture was worn and patched with rawhide. Fargo sat on a high-backed pine settle, pleasantly sandwiched between the Scott sisters.

"Ozark West Transfer," explained "Professor" Dagobert Hastings, "is strictly a short-line operation, as is Anslowe Deacon's Fort Smith Express. We fill the void between three huge operations: Russell, Majors and Waddell to the north, Butterfield Stagecoach Line and Overland Freight to the south."

Hastings was sunken-cheeked and bandy-legged with a whirlwind tangle of white hair and a body like a rumpled pillow. He wore green eyeshades and when Fargo entered the station he was poring over a calfskin-bound accounts ledger. Now he stood before a large wall map, pointing out routes and locations with his ink-stained index finger.

"Butterfield's mail contract is our most lucrative venture," he droned on in his nasal voice. "We pick up the mail at the sorting station in Fayetteville and haul it only as far as West Fork. Butterfield stagecoaches pick it up there and deliver it to all points west."

"I don't get it," Fargo interrupted. "West Fork can't be more than twenty miles south of here. How can there be so much profit in such a short run?"

"Because, sir, thankfully the federal government is run by fools. It's called 'relay compensation.' Any route handled by a subcontractor is worth the same price, regardless of the distance involved. Which, of course, explains Anslowe Deacon's zeal to undermine Ozark West and secure that contract for himself."

"And he's on the verge of succeeding," Marcella Scott interjected in a bitter tone. "Butterfield is an extremely efficient operation, and they won't tolerate inefficiency in their independent contractors."

Fargo knew all about Butterfield Stagecoach Line. He would have preferred that most of this hustle and bustle of "progress" remain east of the Mississippi. But he couldn't help admiring Butterfield's remarkable operation transporting mail from St. Louis to San Francisco. With 280 coaches and eight hundred workers they hauled mail between the two cities in an astounding twenty-two days.

But the Professor and Marcella were dead-on: that impressive schedule depended on the predictable reliability of their various transfer stations. One weak link was like a broken spoke destroying a wheel—and evidently Ozark West was in danger of becoming that broken spoke.

"We also make a profit transferring freight," the Professor said. "That goes down to the bustling transportation center of Van Buren on the bank of the Arkansas River. That, too, we pick up at the freight depot in Fayetteville. However, the driver from this station takes it only as far as our only relay station at Mountainberg."

"That's something else I don't quite savvy," Fargo said, acutely aware that Malinda, seated to his left, was snuggling up against him tighter and tighter. "You just mentioned that Deacon's outfit has their main station right next to the depot. Why is Ozark West three miles away?"

"Filthy politics," Marcella fumed. "The mayor of Fayetteville happens to be Deacon's former business partner. He convinced the city councilmen to pass an ordinance barring Ozark West from building within the city limits. This was the nearest location where Uncle Orrin could buy enough land."

"Just so," Dagobert Hastings said. "However, they cannot stop us from receiving freight and mail. The extra three miles is only a nuisance. Our problem isn't Fayetteville—it's farther south in the aptly named Devil's Den region."

"That Indian stinks," Malinda suddenly spoke up, aiming a withering glance at Cranky Man, who stood nearby, leaning against a wall and looking bored. "Does he have to be in the house? He keeps breaking wind."

"Fox smells his own hole first," Cranky Man replied.

"Devil's Den," the Professor repeated emphatically, irritated at the interruption. "It's the rugged terrain that gives it its name—some of the worst in the entire Ozark region although it is spectacular to behold."

"I know the area," Fargo said in a bored tone. "If you've got a point, don't be afraid to make it."

Dagobert frowned. "My *point*, Mr. Fargo, is that it is ideal for Deacon's mercenaries. Not only does it provide excellent opportunities for ambush attacks, but it is infamous as a magnet for unsavory elements. That makes it more difficult to build a legal case against a specific element."

"Listen . . . Dagobert," Fargo interrupted, trying to keep a straight face as he pronounced the ridiculous name, "you can forget about any damn legal case. I'm no Philadelphia lawyer and this isn't Philadelphia. Marcella hired me to fix this deal, and before it's over it's going to get ugly and bloody."

The Professor surprised him by nodding enthusiastically. "Sir, the moment I saw you I recognized a stout frame and a buoyant spirit. The rugged western type—a 'smasher of foreheads' in biblical parlance. And after all, one cannot make an omelet without first breaking some eggs."

"Fargo don't just break the eggs," Cranky Man quipped. "He kills the chickens and burns down the henhouse."

"A nicely extended metaphor," the Professor said. "Quite impressive in an aborigine."

"You got the wrong tribe," Cranky Man corrected him. "I'm Choctaw."

"You misunderstand. An aborigine is a member of the indigenous population of a region."

"Yeah, that clears it up," the Choctaw said, looking at Fargo and shrugging.

Marcella brazenly stroked Fargo's thigh, forcing him to use his hat to cover the sudden furrow in his buckskins.

"Grub pile," Stan McKinney announced, coming out of the kitchen with two steaming plates. "I'll be back with doughnuts and coffee for the rest."

He set the plates on a trestle table near a side wall. Cranky Man hurried to the table, grabbed a plate, stole a biscuit off Fargo's plate and moved to a chair well away from the table.

24

Fargo and the Professor followed the Scott sisters to the table, Fargo eyeing both of them appreciatively.

"Arrangement and symmetry," the Professor confided in a lowered voice, "were highly prized by the Egyptians. These sisters are exemplars of both."

"Yeah, they're both mighty shapely," Fargo agreed. "If that's what you said."

Fargo tucked into a plate of delicious Irish stew.

"This Anslowe Deacon," he said between bites, "is he the type who scares easy?"

"Anslowe Deacon is a monument to egotism," the Professor replied. "Therefore, the fact that he lacks personal courage will not dissuade him from his ambitions."

"He dresses like those gal-boy fops in Paris," Malinda offered, "and has a Cherokee concubine. Imagine . . . a *white* man choosing to have conjugal relations with an Indian."

"Try it sometime," Cranky Man piped up from across the room, speaking with his mouth full. "I mean, when you're finished with Fargo and the cavalry."

"I *don't* want that disgusting savage in this house!" Malinda burst out.

"I'd say he's quite insightful," Marcella barbed.

"He'll be staying in the hay barn," Fargo quickly assured them. "I just wanted him here for this first meeting. Marcella, what's this business about a missing bracelet and you being out on bail?"

Her nostrils flared. "It's one more of Deacon's filthy ploys! A few weeks back we had two passengers, a wealthy couple from Kansas City who wanted to board a Butterfield stage at West Fork. They had to spend the night here. The woman had a magnificent emerald-and-diamond bracelet worth thousands. I locked it in a sturdy drawer in the office for safekeeping.

"During the night it disappeared. The woman pressed charges against me and a Fayetteville constable arrested me. Dagobert represented me at the arraignment and managed to get me out of jail on a five-hundred-dollar bond."

"I really didn't know what I was doing," the Professor admitted. "But the judge granted the bond to shut me up."

"But in two weeks," Marcella added, "my case goes to trial. And given the corrupt judiciary in Fayetteville, I may well go to a woman's penitentiary unless I can prove who took that bracelet."

"The sheriff," Fargo said, sopping up gravy with a biscuit, "mentioned something else that was stolen? Something important to you?"

Marcella's pretty face turned a light pink. "Yes."

She made no effort to amplify the answer, and Fargo, despite his curiosity, let the topic die a natural death.

"Before I do anything else," Fargo decided, "I'm going to pay a little visit to Anslowe Deacon. Sounds like he's the head of the snake."

"Work quickly, Mr. Fargo," the Professor urged. "To put it succinctly, we're wandering from pillar to post."

Fargo's eyebrows rose. "Would you mind spelling that out plain, Dagobert?"

"I mean simply that we're suffering one difficulty after another, and if this continues Ozark West will be run out of business."

The Professor dropped unpleasant subjects and next held forth at length on somebody he called "the mighty Viceroys of Kush," but Fargo didn't even pretend to listen, devouring several doughnuts with gusto while Malinda played footsie with him under the table.

"It's getting late," Marcella finally announced, "and I'll have to drive into town early to hire a new driver. Mr. Fargo, the workers all have rooms off the hallway through that door behind you. You'll find yours at the end."

"I'll show him," Malinda volunteered.

"He can find it on his own," Marcella snapped.

Cranky Man had already headed outside. He stopped with his hand on the latchstring and turned back around.

"Hey, Malinda? Wanna come out to the barn with me and show me my stall? Maybe we could even *horse* around."

"You're filthy and disgusting!"

Cranky Man laughed, stuck his tongue out at her and wiggled it suggestively, then went outside.

5

The annoying whistle of a bobwhite, right outside his window, woke Fargo just as the sun began to rise.

The unaccustomed comfort of a feather mattress had caused him to sleep later than he'd intended. Even when sleeping indoors, Fargo had a long-ingrained habit to lie still and listen after waking up. Occasional sharp whistles, and the protesting squeal of mules, told him that Stan McKinney was already at work wrangling teams into the traces.

Fargo usually slept in his clothing. He sat up, wrestled his boots on, grabbed his gun belt off a bedpost and buckled it on. His bladder ached insistently, but before he headed outside to relieve himself he picked his binoculars up from atop a narrow highboy and moved to the small bedroom's single sash window. He had already propped his Henry against the wall nearby.

He tugged the window open and knelt with his elbows on the sill, focusing the binoculars and beginning to elevate and traverse the densely wooded hills looming over the small valley.

The grisly image of Jimbo Miller's shattered skull was still clear in his mind. And since Fargo never dismissed anything as coincidence, so were Eb Scofield and his intimidating Sharps Big Fifty. But if a shooter was holed up somewhere in those forested hills, Fargo knew it would be like trying to spot a sliver in an elephant's ass.

He searched patiently and thoroughly but spotted nothing that didn't belong to the terrain. Fargo was about to lower the glasses when a flock of birds suddenly squirted up from the trees.

Unless startled, Fargo knew from long observation, birds

27

tended to rise in a quick sequence and then settle into a flight pattern. These had taken flight helter-skelter.

Fargo fine-focused and closely studied the area where they'd been startled.

A human face flickered into view, then disappeared.

Could be a hunter, Fargo reminded himself. Arkansas hill dwellers spent little time in stores. Again the face flickered into view, and this time Fargo spotted the familiar lizard eyes.

But the Trailsman needed a landmark close to Scofield to orient himself once he traded the spyglasses for his Henry. He spotted one: a lightning-split tree with a high fork.

Fargo jacked a round into the sixteen-shot Henry's chamber and laid the long barrel across the sill, moving the sights an inch to the left of the tree. He squeezed off his first shot and continued working the lever, filling the quiet house with a sudden, hammering racket of gunfire.

Shell casings clanged to the puncheon floor, a woman screamed, and male shouts and curses erupted. Fargo emptied half the tube magazine and laid his rifle aside, snatching up the binoculars again.

He grinned when he momentarily glimpsed Eb Scofield retreating in headlong panic. Fargo knew odds were long that he had hit him, but the Scofield boys might think twice before sending out the next sniper around the station.

Stan McKinney's voice sounded from the doorway. "What in blue blazes . . . ?"

Fargo stood up and stretched the kinks out of his back. "Just a little visit from Eb Scofield."

Marcella, her face white as new linen, peered around McKinney. The room was filled with acrid gray-white powder smoke.

"You don't waste any time bringing down the thunder, do you, Mr. Fargo?"

"Best way to cure a boil is to lance it," Fargo replied cheerfully.

Malinda squeezed into the doorway beside her sister wearing only a thin muslin chemise. Fargo admired the fulsome dents where her nipples pressed into the fabric. Nor did he miss the dark, exciting, triangular outline of her nether bush.

"Good morning, Skye," chirped her melodic voice.

Fargo grinned. "It certainly is now."

"Go get dressed, Lady Godiva," Marcella snapped. "Breakfast is ready, Mr. Fargo, if you're done waking up the snakes. Malinda and I have only tea in the morning, in my office, so I'll speak with you later."

A disgruntled Cranky Man, still sleep drunk, appeared outside the window, straw stuck in his hair.

"I mighta known," he groused, spotting the smoke and all the spent shell casings. "When do we eat?"

"I'll send Cecil out with a plate," Marcella said stiffly. "*And* a lump of soap."

"'Preciate the soap," the Choctaw replied. "I'll soften my saddle with it."

Everyone left and Fargo reloaded the Henry's magazine. Stan, Cecil and the Professor were seated at the breakfast table along with two new faces.

"Skye," the affable stock tender said, "meet Sebastian Kilroy. He's a dang fine whip-cracker when he's sober. And he knows so many jokes, he could fill a book with 'em. This other jasper with the frown on his face is Lonny Munro, our blacksmith and wheelwright. Good harness mender, too."

Fargo gave both men a quick size-up. Kilroy was an old mossy horn with a stout, muscular body turning to fat. Munro seemed taciturn and indifferent, a homely, jut-jawed man who appeared to have little use for the world around him.

"Glad to make your acquaintance," Fargo said, shoving his long legs under the table and attacking a plate of eggs and scrapple.

"Well, Mr. Fargo," the Professor remarked, "your first morning with us and we wake up to the proverbial hail of gunfire. As I told Marcella last night, a man like you lives by the Code of Hammurabi: an eye for an eye, a tooth for a tooth."

"Not really, Dagobert," Fargo countered. "If a man cost me an eye on purpose, I'd kill him. I need my eyes."

"I reckon you've stopped lead a few times," Sebastian said.

"Arrows, knives, spears and hatchet blades, too. I've had rocks and frying pans bounced off my head, bombs explode under me, rock salt in my ass, and every manner of whip strip my hide. And one winter up in Dakota a woman flogged me with a frozen cat. Yet none of it has pounded any sense into me."

Fargo noticed Cecil ignoring his own breakfast to stare at Fargo as if he were the best act in the circus.

"Eat up, son," Fargo urged the kid. "And don't pay any attention to my boasting."

"I bet all of it's true, Mr. Fargo," the kid said. "I've read all about you in books, and books ain't allowed to lie."

Sebastian snorted. "Rock this one to sleep, Mother."

"Cecil here," Stan cut in, "wants to move out to Texas and become a ranger."

"Then he best eat his breakfast," Fargo said. "Those old boys are strong."

The kid tied into his food while Fargo turned his attention to Sebastian. "You the only driver at this station?"

"I am at the moment, but we had three at one time. Jimbo was cut down yesterday, and another quit a week ago after his wagon was fired on for the second time down in Devil's Den. Miss Scott is driving into town this morning to hire on a teamster named Jeremiah Pullman."

"Sebastian keeps the mail flowing," Stan explained, "but our freight is piling up."

"Men are quitting at our relay station in Mountainberg, too," Sebastian said. "Scared spitless. Anslowe Deacon and his skunk-bit coyotes aim to tangle our twine, all right."

"I'll be paying Deacon a little visit this morning," Fargo said. "A little courtesy call, you might say."

Dagobert cleared his throat. "The entire history of human civilization, gentlemen, has been summed up by a pithy ancient: 'They were born, they suffered, they died.'"

Everyone ignored him. Lonny Munro, Fargo noticed, hadn't spoken a word or even looked up from his plate. But then, plenty of men kept to themselves, a trait that had never bothered Fargo.

"Did you boys hear," Sebastian piped up, "about the woman that tried to kill a man with a look? She was cross-eyed and ended up killing the man next to him."

Stan McKinney sprayed food when he burst out laughing.

"See what I mean, Skye? Sebastian is a caution to screech owls."

"Yeah," Fargo said from a deadpan, "that was a corker, all right."

Right after breakfast Sebastian Kilroy's Concord swift wagon rolled out of the yard headed for the mail-and-freight depot in Fayetteville. Fargo, leery of that outhouse death chamber, relieved himself behind the hay barn, then went inside.

Cranky Man had already saddled both horses and now lay in the straw, digesting his breakfast and smoking his clay pipe.

"I take it that was a Scofield you were plinking at this morning," he greeted Fargo.

"Eb Scofield, to chew it fine. I got a hunch he meant to plug me when I went out to the crapper."

"That bunch seems to like shithouses."

Fargo checked the Ovaro's hooves for cracks or stone bruises, then carefully felt all four legs for signs of tendon problems. He led the pinto up and down the barn.

Cranky Man nodded his approval. His knowledge of horses was prodigious, and he was the only man Fargo knew of who could sneak up on the Ovaro at night and keep him quiet while rifling Fargo's saddlebags.

"If a horse walks good he'll gallop good," the Choctaw said. "That baldy of mine is ugly as a baboon's ass, but the first time I seen him walk I knew I had to steal him."

"I see you still tote that New Haven Arms percussion gun," Fargo said, glancing at the old cork-gripped revolver jammed into Cranky Man's waistband.

"Take a closer look," Cranky Man said, handing the weapon to Fargo.

Fargo noticed right off that the nib for holding percussion caps had been filed off. He swung the wheel out and saw that it had been rechambered for self-contained cartridges.

"Nice work," Fargo said. "But you couldn't hit a bull in the butt with a banjo anyway. It was your knife that saved my life at Lead Hill. You still got it?"

Cranky Man reached behind his neck where a sheath was

sewn under the collar of his shirt. He pulled out the narrow-bladed throwing knife.

"Good," Fargo said. "You saved my bacon once with that blade, and what man has done man can do. Let's dust our hocks toward Fayetteville."

The two men avoided the wagon road Sebastian had taken, wending through the trees beside it, which had been thinned out by lumber seekers. Stan had informed Fargo that Anslowe Deacon lived in rooms at the rear of the Fort Smith Express Company office on Commerce Street.

Under the watchful, suspicious eyes of two workers, they swung around the busy wagon yard into an alley behind the big frame building.

"Those two in the yard," Cranky Man remarked as they dismounted, "weren't too damn happy 'bout seeing a redskin toting a short iron."

"The way you say," Fargo agreed, slipping rawhide hobbles on the Ovaro. "We best keep this visit short and sweet."

Fargo thumped on the alley door with the side of his fist. It was opened by a pretty Cherokee woman wearing an embroidered buckskin dress. She sized up Fargo with mistrustful eyes.

"I want to see Deacon," Fargo told her.

"Not here."

She tried to shut the door but Fargo wedged it with his foot.

"I'll just see for myself," he said, forcing the door open wider.

In an amazing blur of speed the Cherokee produced a bone-handled obsidian knife. She came within a whisker of gutting Fargo with it before he managed to knock her arm aside with a left forearm block and trap her arm by the wrist.

But that didn't stop the determined squaw. Fargo yowled in pain when she sank her teeth deep into his hand while simultaneously kicking his shins repeatedly.

The teeth sank deeper into his left hand as she clamped on like a bulldog. Faced with no other choice, Fargo tossed a short, fast punch into the side of her jaw, knocking her out cold.

"Good job," Cranky Man roweled from behind him.

"Maybe you can beat the shit out of a couple of babies before we leave town."

"Sew up your lips and put that hellcat under the gun," Fargo ordered. "Christ, she damn near bit my hand off."

While Cranky Man stood guard over the Cherokee, Fargo shucked out his Colt and moved farther into the well-furnished living quarters. A cloying, sickly-sweet odor of lavender tickled his nostrils.

Spotting no one else in the room off the alley, Fargo entered a short hallway and tried the first door. It opened onto a luxuriously appointed bedroom with a tester bed and mahogany furnishings. A man in a fancy ruffled shirt and octagonal necktie stood primping in front of a cheval glass. The lavender smell was even stronger now, and Fargo realized the man was wearing powerful cologne.

He started violently when Fargo pushed in, turning away from the mirror to stare at the buckskin-clad intruder.

"Is this a robbery?"

"Anslowe Deacon?"

The man nodded. He had piercing dark eyes, a hawk nose, a high pompadour and fleshy lips the color of raw liver.

"You have the advantage on me, Mr. . . . ?"

"Fargo. Skye Fargo. So you're the perfumed puff who employs the Scofield boys."

"I don't know who you're talking about. What's the purpose of this intrusion?"

"Bad money drives out good," Fargo said. "That's what it's about. And your plan is to drive out the Scott sisters any way you can."

"You must be smoking tar balls. I—"

"Shut up," Fargo said. "You've already killed Orrin Scott and Jimbo Miller. I don't take too kindly to that, and I plan to do some killing of my own."

"Fargo, this is all riddles to me. I don't—"

"Just a safety tip," Fargo pressed on. "You'd better think real deep and come to Jesus before he comes to you and covers you with a blanket."

"Is that threat or prophecy, Mr. Fargo?"

"Call it Cajun sassafras for all I care. You heard me."

"Be very careful not to step in something you can't wipe off."

"That's rich," Fargo said, "coming from a . . . man who hides behind squaws."

"Yes, I noticed your bloody hand. Morning Star is very loyal to me. But I assure you I have far more resources."

"Yeah. And like I said—I plan to do some killing."

Deacon turned back to the mirror and continued fussing with his tie. "I've heard of you, Fargo. You know, in one respect we're both alike: we're both independent contractors. So why don't you go for the highest bidder? I'll double whatever those two twats are paying you."

"I don't work for men who wear perfume to cover up their cowardly stink," Fargo said. "And this little conversation has gone as far as it can go. This is the last warning you'll get from me. If I look you up again, it'll be to sink an air shaft through you."

Fargo leathered his six-gun and returned to the front room. Morning Star had revived and now sat on the floor, watching Fargo with the eyes of a sullen animal.

"Sorry I had to clout you," Fargo told her. "But don't try to put that frog-sticker in me again. Let's vamoose, Cranky Man."

They emerged into the bright morning sunshine and moved toward their horses.

"Both you sons-a-bitches, *freeze*!"

The two men who had watched them from the wagon yard earlier now stepped around the corner of the building. And the first thing Fargo noticed were the twin, unblinking eyes of a sawed-off scattergun staring right at him.

6

"Don't say a word or make a play," Fargo muttered to Cranky Man. "We don't want to stir up Indian fever."

"Make a play? Christ, Fargo, my nuts just rolled under the porch."

"Shut your filthy sewers," ordered the worker with the scattergun. "Use just your thumbs and *one* finger to ease them barking irons out. Then drop 'em. Try any parlor tricks"—he wagged the barrels of the sawed-off—"and they'll have to bury you two with a rake."

Both men complied. The other worker held a Smith & Wesson revolver trained on them.

"You—the red Arab," snarled the one with the revolver at Cranky Man. "The hell you doing heeled? It's agin the law."

"He can't speak any English," Fargo said.

"Well, now, Indian lover, what the hell you doin' running around chummy with a buck?"

Scattergun said, "I'm thinking these two must be sweet on each other, Hoby."

"There you go—that's it. These boys must like the pole, not the hole. Tell me, sister-boy: which one pitches and which one catches?"

"You know, it's funny," Fargo said, "that you two backwoods crackers would go right to that line of thinking. Think about such things a lot, do you?"

Hoby's bloated red face twisted even meaner. "Well now, Indian lover—I take serious exception to them words."

"I figured you might. That's why I said 'em."

"You're sniffin' the wrong dog's butt, mister," Hoby assured him. "And you just inked your own death warrant."

35

While all this went forward Fargo's mind was desperately trying to scratch out a plan of action.

"The hell you doing back there bothering the boss?" Scattergun demanded.

"We came to see him about jobs," Fargo said. "I used to whip freight wagons for the army, and this half-breed is a crackerjack wrangler."

"That's one big load of goat shit, Indian lover. The hell's your name?"

Fargo, his mind still rapidly calculating, glanced at the door leading into Deacon's quarters. He recalled his violent reception minutes ago. Right now Morning Star was likely still wound tighter than an eight-day clock.

The odds were long, but he recalled his credo: *Always mislead, mystify and surprise your enemies.*

"Crawford Miller," Fargo replied.

Two more of Deacon's workers stepped around the corner.

"Miller?" Scattergun slanted an uneasy glance toward Hoby. "Any relation to Jimbo Miller?"

"He was my brother," Fargo replied. "And if you're wondering why you didn't hear a gunshot, glom the toothpick in my boot."

"Jesus Christ with a wooden dick!" Hoby exclaimed. "Keep 'em covered, Steve!"

Hoby shot toward the door and jerked it open. Moments later a hideous scream reverberated down the alley when the Cherokee's knife pierced his lights. He collapsed backward into the alley, blood spuming.

This was Fargo's opportunity and he didn't waste it. He knelt quickly to scoop up his Colt while Steve stared in numb shock at his friend. Fargo shot him in both kneecaps, adding to the chorus of bloodcurdling screams and sending the scattergun into the dirt when Steve fell face forward.

Before the two latest arrivals could react, Fargo leveled his still-smoking Colt on them.

"You boys want the balance of these pills?"

Evidently neither man wanted to be dosed. Both fled back around the corner of the building.

"Sift sand!" Fargo called to Cranky Man, knocking the Ovaro's hobbles loose and vaulting into the saddle.

They quickly rated their mounts up to a gallop, the Ovaro's irons thundering as the two men fled toward the outskirts of town even as a crackling volley of gunfire erupted behind them.

"I understand your reason for confronting Deacon," Marcella Scott said, her pretty face apprehensive. "But one of his workers is dead and another probably crippled—and Deacon has influence in Fayetteville. If he brings the law into this, Mr. Fargo, it could get ugly."

"It could. But I didn't kill that worker," Fargo reminded her. "As for the one I plugged in the knees—Arkansas may be a state, but this far west it's still the frontier. Wounding a man is no great shakes."

"Perhaps so, but what's to prevent Deacon from putting the killing on you?"

"He might, and if he does, me and Cranky Man will just have to take to the woods. We both know how to avoid the law—especially these soft-handed townies. But I don't think Deacon *will* go to law."

"And why not?"

It was late morning and Fargo, Marcella and Dagobert Hastings sat in Marcella's office while Fargo made his report.

"Because," Fargo replied, "influence or no, Deacon is up to his eyeballs in murder and other crimes, and he's got more planned. Owning the judge doesn't mean you own the jury. He's the take-charge type and 'pears to me he's confident in his dirt workers. Why risk having the law turn on you like a rabid dog if you figure you can handle the deal on your own?"

"Sound reasoning," Dagobert agreed.

Marcella nodded. "Yes, I see your point. But don't forget that I am already in trouble with the law over that stolen bracelet."

"Yes, my dear," Dagobert said, "and no doubt one of Deacon's minions stole it. But Deacon did not bring that case before the bar—Mrs. Truella Brubaker did."

"I know, but Deacon is aware of my legal problem. Since I'm already under indictment for one crime, he might—"

"Look, lady," Fargo cut in, "the ox is in the ditch, so don't fret the law. The best way to clear you of that charge *and* the threat from Deacon is to take the bull by the horns and throw it hard."

"That's a mixed metaphor," the Professor pointed out. "You began with an ox and concluded with a bull."

"Dagobert," Marcella snapped impatiently, "never mind the pedantry. Mr. Fargo is making his points clearly. And those bite marks on his hand suggest that metaphors are hardly his problem."

A rattling crash of pots and pans sounded from the slope-off kitchen attached to the station house.

"Excuse me," Marcella said, rising from behind her desk. "Malinda is cooking and that usually spells disaster."

Fargo and Dagobert politely stood as she left the room. Fargo admired the wasp-waisted beauty as she retreated.

Dagobert chuckled. "I certainly cannot fault a virile young man like yourself for desiring . . . a biological adventure with either of those beautiful sisters."

"A biological adventure?" Fargo repeated as he folded back into a spindle-back chair. "Look, Professor, nix on the thirty-five-cent words. I'm not a schoolman."

"And a good thing for us. Mr. Fargo, for most of human civilization there is no written record. Those that have been left are mostly lies. A man who has been to Harvard simply knows more lies than a man who hasn't."

Fargo waved this piffle aside as if shooing a fly. Marcella returned, flour clinging to the tip of her nose.

"That girl," she fumed. "She can't keep her mind on the simplest things once a desirable man enters the picture. I wish you were homely, Mr. Fargo."

"Well, I'm glad you and your sister aren't."

She gave him a brief, distracted smile. "You said something about a night guard?"

Fargo nodded. "From sunset to sunup. Did you hire that new driver this morning?"

"Yes, Jeremiah Pullman. He's rather a surly man, but he's an experienced teamster and he's already on the job picking up backlogged freight."

"Good, that's one more sentry. Toss me and Cranky Man into the mix along with Pullman, Sebastian, Stan and Lonny Munro. That's six guards, each standing a two-hour watch."

"What course of action do you have planned next?" Dagobert asked.

"I'll spend the rest of this day scouting the area around here to get the lay of the land. The Scofields already know every inch of it, but I need to fix some local landmarks, escape routes and such in my mind before I can hope to tangle with them."

Fargo pushed out of the chair. "But I also want to get a size-up on these five Scofield boys. The only one I can recognize is Eb. Stan told me they spend plenty of time in the Hog's Breath saloon in Busted Flush, so me and Stan will head there after supper so he can maybe point some out to me. I've already paid my respects to their boss. Now it's their turn."

"Mr. Fargo," Marcella said as Fargo turned to leave. "May I speak with you for a moment—privately?"

Dagobert got the hint and left the office.

"There's something I haven't told you yet," Marcella said, standing up and stepping away from the desk. "Would you please take a look under the desk?"

Marcella tugged her chair aside and Fargo tucked in front of the kneehole.

"The locked drawer I mentioned," she explained, "is in fact a carefully hidden *secret* drawer. Pull that small brass ring on the bottom of the desktop. It's hard to spot, but you'll feel it."

Fargo felt around until his fingers encountered the ring. He tugged down on it and a narrow drawer slid almost silently open at a right angle to the other drawers.

"You can't even see it unless you know it's there and look under the desk," Fargo remarked.

He pushed it shut again. "It's built so well, you can hardly even see a seam when it's shut. So it wasn't really *broken* into?"

"Exactly," she confirmed in a miserable tone. "Which means two things: First, it will appear in court that I *had* to take that bracelet because the drawer is so hard to spot. And second, since I'm not the thief, it seems almost certain that the real thief either works here or was told about that drawer by someone who works here—although it's also possible an Ozark West

39

employee indiscreetly mentioned it to an outsider and the word got to the wrong ears."

"It's a poser," Fargo agreed. "Who knows about it besides you?"

"Well, Dagobert and Malinda for certain. But Uncle Orrin was very trusting of his workers. Any of them, including any who have since quit, could know."

"No offense, but you know your sister better than I do. Could she have taken that bracelet? It sounds like something a woman would love."

"She did admire it greatly," Marcella replied. "But so do I, and as you said, any woman would. It's absolutely stunning."

Marcella mulled it for a few moments. "Malinda is hardly a paragon of virtue and she does resent me—we aren't as close as sisters ought to be. But I don't think she'd send me to a penitentiary for it."

"How 'bout Dagobert?"

"My uncle trusted him implicitly and so do I. Nor does he seem to value money greatly. His books are his greatest treasures."

"I'll shake the bushes," Fargo said, "and see what falls out. But there've been two murders so far and other crimes. If we can clear those up we might get to the bottom of this bracelet deal, too."

Fargo watched her face closely and added, "Are you sure you don't want to tell me what else was stolen?"

Again Marcella flushed a slight pink.

"Speaking of my sister," she said, awkwardly changing the subject, "it may appear to you that she will be an easy conquest."

She paused, but Fargo said nothing.

"She has cocked her eye at you, all right," Marcella forged on, "but her long game has just begun."

"Her long game?"

"Yes. She will certainly move heaven and earth to be alone with you. But the truth is, she's a shameless tease. She appears sweet, to men, but in fact she is cruel. It excites her immensely to . . . arouse a man to a fever pitch and then dash his hopes. I just thought you should know that."

Fargo nodded. "What about you, Marcella? Are you a tease, too?"

That hair-trigger indignation ignited in her gorgeous green eyes.

"No, Mr. Fargo, definitely not. I am what disappointed men call a cold fish. Your good looks and rugged masculinity are wasted on me. You are my employee and nothing more."

Fargo's lips twitched into a grin. "Well, it's always the lady's choice with me. But you sure are pretty when you get on your high horse. And you can't hang a man for his thoughts."

"You're welcome to your thoughts. But please control your actions where I'm concerned. As for my sister, you—"

A string of distant gunshots crackled, stopping Marcella in midsentence.

"Fargo!" Stan McKinney's bullhorn voice bellowed. "We got bad trouble out here!"

7

The scene in the corral was bedlam.

Several mules lay dead or dying and the rest were squealing and braying in a panic, the gunshots having thrown them into a confused mill.

The shots continued unabated, and as Fargo burst out of the station he watched dust puff up from a mule's flank as a bullet brought it buckling to its knees. McKinney, ably assisted by Cranky Man, was trying to wrangle the agitated animals back into the stock sheds.

"Keep the mules between your bodies and the hills to the east!" Fargo shouted above the raucous din.

Fargo spotted distant powder smoke and moved to a stone water trough, dropping into a kneeling-offhand position. For the second time that day he set to work firing into the hills, patterning his shots to strike just beneath the gray-white haze rising from the hills.

After his fifth or sixth shot the firing from the hills slowed. But only when the Henry's magazine was nearly empty, and heat radiated from the long barrel, did the fusillade end.

Five mules lay in the corral, two dead and three mortally wounded. Fargo drew his Colt and dispatched the three with head shots, his face grim at the distasteful task.

"Hell 'n' furies!" McKinney said. "From now on I'll have to keep them hemmed in the sheds. And I'll play hell dragging the dead ones outta here."

He looked at Cranky Man. "You saved several of those mules, Crotchety Man. You're a damn good wrangler."

"It's *Cranky* Man," the Choctaw reminded him. "I'll help you drag them out, but we're not going to waste all that mule meat. You can butcher some tasty steaks from them."

Dagobert, young Cecil, Lonny Munro—the taciturn wheel-wright and blacksmith—and the Scott sisters had congregated in the yard.

"Don't cluster in the open like that," Fargo snapped. "All of you put something between you and those hills. This attack on the mules could just be a lure."

"I'm afraid, Mr. Fargo," said Marcella, who had obedi-ently moved out of the line of fire, "that this may be retalia-tion for your escapade this morning in Fayetteville."

"Distinct possibility," Fargo agreed, thumbing reloads into his Colt. "But I warned you last night it was gonna get rough and ugly. If you want peace and harmony, hire a preacher."

She shook her head. "No, I believe I hired the right man."

"Yes, my dear," Dagobert threw in. "We must pass through the bitter waters before we reach the sweet. As Plato once observed—"

"Oh, turn off the tap!" said Malinda, who had never warmed up to the Professor. She sent Fargo another of her promissory, cheek-cracking smiles.

Fargo recalled Marcella's judgment about her sister: *It excites her immensely to arouse a man to a fever pitch and then dash his hopes.*

We'll see about that, Fargo thought. She wouldn't be the first tease to end up lipping salt from Skye Fargo's callused hand.

"Anybody here happen to know where the Scofields hole up?" Fargo asked.

"The three brothers got a cabin somewhere in the hills, is all I know," Stan replied. "According to bubbling hearsay, they killed the owner and took it over. The two cousins, Lem and Bubba, got a shebang somewhere close by."

Fargo tacked the Ovaro and rode out alone for several hours to make the "mind maps" that made him the most sought-after civilian scout for the U.S. Army—mind maps that had saved his bacon more than once.

Using Ozark West station as a hub, he rode in ever-expanding circles, noting everything from coverts and tan-gled deadfalls to caves and old game traces once used by now displaced Indians. He spotted several cabins and shacks but rode wide of them for now.

That night at supper Fargo met the newly hired driver,

Jeremiah Pullman. He was a type Fargo had met often on the frontier: surly and resentful, as if life had given him the go-by and the next guy was always a prick.

"Nobody said squat to me about standing guard nights," he complained when Dagobert Hastings posted the sentry schedule beside the main door of the station.

"It won't be permanent," Fargo assured him. "I'm taking a stint, too."

"If there's gonna be lead-chucking, we oughta draw fightin' wages," he insisted.

Fargo, knowing how badly Marcella needed whip-crackers, kept his tone level. "I'll talk to Miss Scott about it," he lied.

"Get over your peeve, new man," Sebastian Kilroy growled at Pullman. "This ain't Delaware. There're times when a man has to face danger."

"The guard runs from six at night until six in the morning," Fargo explained. "The Professor here has volunteered his timepiece. Each man wakes up his relief and gives him the watch."

"Why don't that spindly-legged, book-spouting fool have to walk guard?" Pullman carped.

"He's a desk soldier," Fargo said quickly before an indignant Dagobert could start gasbagging.

"I ain't a desk soldier, Mr. Fargo," spoke up Cecil. "How's come I ain't on the guard?"

"If you're serious 'bout joining up with the Texas Rangers," Fargo replied, "you've got to get your sleep while your bones are still growing."

Cecil, who slept on a pallet in the hay barn, said, "Yessir. But I don't get no sleep anyhow with that Injun out there. He snores so loud, he even wakes up the horses. He—"

"The calf don't bellow to the bull," Fargo cut him off, ending the matter.

After supper Fargo took a plate and a cup of coffee out to Cranky Man.

"I'm heading into town with Stan and Sebastian," Fargo said. "Silas won't let you into the Hog's Breath, and I need to track down this Scofield bunch and see what they look like, maybe find out where they stay."

"Staying right here suits me," Cranky Man said. "Get me a bottle, wouldja?"

"Maybe. You got guard duty tonight from ten to midnight. The new driver will roust you—don't knife him. I'm your relief. Just come by my window at two o'clock. Can you read a timepiece?"

"Yeah, numbers I can read. But listen, Fargo, why'n't we just haul ass outta here? We was damn near killed today—our *first* day on the job."

Fargo grinned. "Yeah. It's a privilege to be here, ain't it?"

The three men from Ozark West Transfer arrived in Busted Flush about a half hour after sunset. At least a dozen horses and mules were lined up at the hitch rail out front of the Hog's Breath, bridles down.

Fargo noticed that a crude repair job had been done on the hole where Deputy Harney Roscoe had flown through the wall. He slapped the batwings and immediately breathed in the familiar saloon odor of sweat, tobacco, grain mash, leather and the cheap perfume used by soiled doves.

"Oh, Christ," Silas the bartender said when he saw Fargo and his companions belly up to the bar. "Fargo, I just got that wall fixed today. *Don't* tear the place up again."

"I'll be a scrubbed angel," Fargo promised, although in fact he had already spotted Eb Scofield and two other men at a table near the back wall.

"What's yours, gents?" Silas asked.

"Three jolts off the top shelf," Stan said, planking two silver dollars on the bar. "First one's on me, boys."

Fargo used the back-bar mirror to study the trio at Scofield's table. Sebastian saw him looking.

"You struck a bonanza, Fargo," he said. "Them's the three Scofield brothers. The hairy brute with the little pig eyes is Romer."

"I see he totes a Greener."

"Yeah. The skinny one wearing the Colt Navy way below his hip is Stanton. Folks say he controls all five of the Scofield boys. Like you can see, he fancies himself a gun-thrower."

All three men were staring unrelentingly at Fargo's back.

45

Silas noticed this, and Fargo watching the mirror, and didn't like what he was seeing.

"Say, boys," he coaxed, "why not try your luck in the back room? The roulette wheel has been running hot."

Fargo grinned. He already knew that the Hog's Breath had the usual percentage rig on the games, so the house generally won.

"Calm down, Silas," he said. "I'm not looking to get jugged again."

"Fargo," Sebastian said, "you know what a rabbi is?"

"A Jewish preacher, ain't he?"

"Yeah. Well, see, this priest and this rabbi are passengers on a stagecoach. The priest says, 'Say, how come rabbis never eat ham?' And the rabbi tells him, 'Well, it's against our religion. How come you priests won't sleep with women?' And the priest says, 'Oh, my, that's against *our* religion.'

"So the rabbi says, 'Well I'll tell you what. You oughta try pussy sometime. It's a helluva lot better than ham.' "

This one threw Stan into stitches. Fargo chuckled politely but kept his eyes on the mirror. Something was brewing at the Scofield table.

"Speaking of pussy," Sebastian said to Fargo, "that little tart Malinda's got her cap set for you—her nightcap."

"She's mighty easy on the eyes," Stan said.

"Listen," Sebastian said. "After staring at mules' butts all day long, any female looks good."

"Steady on, boys," Fargo spoke up. "Here comes Eb with the opening volley."

"Fargo, *don't* tear my saloon down," Silas begged.

Eb Scofield sauntered up to the spot next to Fargo. His lizard eyes stared unblinking into Fargo's.

"Listen, bitch, light a shuck while you still can or get your tombstone carved. You ain't got a Chinaman's chance. You screwed the pooch good when you crossed Anslowe Deacon this morning."

"You know, Eb," Fargo said amiably, "when a man calls me bitch, I start to hear wedding bells. Does this mean I'm spoken for?"

Whatever Scofield had expected, this wasn't it. Some of his bravado crumbled into confusion.

"You heard what I said, Fargo."

"I certainly did, and I'm the happiest man in Arkansas. When can I expect the ring?"

This was too much for Eb, who left abruptly and returned to his table. Silas had heard all this and now joined Stan and Sebastian in paroxysms of mirth.

"Fargo," he said, "you sure's hell flummoxed that sheep humper."

"Well, I had to spare your saloon," Fargo said. "I just hope he doesn't publish the banns."

The batwings swung open hard and two men stepped into the saloon.

"Well, Fargo, the gang's all here," Stan announced. "That big half-wit-looking son of a buck is Bubba Scofield."

"The one you suspect murdered Orrin Scott?"

"The very man. The other one is his brother, Lemuel. People say he likes to start fires when he's got a score to settle."

"Hell, is that a *rat* poking out of Bubba's shirt pocket?" Sebastian asked.

Silas nodded, busy wiping up bar slops with a dirty rag. "Ain't it the shits? He talks to it and feeds it like it was his young'un. Mister, them Scofields sleep too many to a bed."

The two new arrivals joined their kin at the table. As if he was following Bubba and Lem, Sheriff Dub Gillycuddy entered the saloon and bellied up beside Fargo.

"You didn't waste any time stirring up the shit, didja?" he greeted the Trailsman. "Word's out 'bout what happened this morning in Fayetteville."

"Any warrants going out?"

"Haven't heard of any. But, Fargo, you best stop leading with your chin. Anslowe Deacon's got crooked friends in high places, and a writ of habeas corpus don't mean shit in Fayetteville. They could lock you up and toss the key and wait for you to go crazy from cooped-up fever, then shoot you for a mad dog."

"Your advice makes a heap of sense, I reckon," Fargo agreed.

"But you plan to ignore it, right?"

Fargo grinned but didn't answer.

The sheriff shook his head in wonder. "It ain't the heat—it's the stupidity. All right, Fargo, but I'm telling you: Deacon aims to spike your hide to the barn door, and he'll pay whatever it takes to do it."

"He bleeds like all the rest. Dub, where do these Scofields hole up?"

"Stanton, Romer and Eb took over the old Peatross cabin in Blue Holler. That's about a thirty-minute ride due north of town. It's a low, brushy hollow with a small creek running through it."

"This cabin—is there a caved-in springhouse over the creek right behind it?"

The sheriff nodded.

"I know right where it is," Fargo said. "Rode past it earlier today. What about Bubba and Lem?"

"That I don't rightly know. They got a shebang somewheres close to the other three, and I'm told it's pretty well hid a-purpose. But all five of those peckerwoods also spend a mort of time farther south in Devil's Den. They know the whole region real good. That's rough country, and if you have to tangle with them there, it'll be a hell buster."

"Yeah, I know the place some. But I plan to make a thorough scout there real soon. If I was a murdering dog, that's where I'd feel safest pulling off my crimes."

"Well, you best cover your ampersand, Trailsman," the sheriff warned as he turned to leave. "The Scofield boys are meaner than Satan with a sunburn. And Anslowe Deacon may dress and smell like a nancy, but he's got a lump of clay where his heart oughta be."

"You two," Fargo said to Stan and Sebastian after the sheriff had gone, "had best skedaddle. Remember, you'll be losing two hours sleep tonight on guard duty."

"Christsakes," Silas said in a disgusted tone, "that big galoot Bubba is playing kissy-face with that filthy black sewer rat. He's crazy as a pet coon."

"What's your plan, Fargo?" Stan asked as he picked his hat up from the bar.

"To fight fire with fire," Fargo replied. "See you later, boys."

8

It had been a long, eventful day and Fargo would dearly have welcomed the soft bed back at the station—and maybe a warm woman to improve his dreams.

But sleep and pleasant dreams would have to wait a bit longer. The Scofield boys had attacked twice today, and Eb had just threatened his life. And clearly they were hatching a new scheme even now—Fargo knew they planned to follow him the moment he left.

Fargo's preferred option would have been to kill all five of them and be rid of the vermin. Just plug the bastards right now from the bar.

But this was an organized state, not a territory. And Sheriff Gillycuddy was right: Fargo was an outsider and most folks around Busted Flush were hill folks who didn't much cotton to outsiders—especially newspaper heroes like Fargo who started depopulating the locals, even the hated ones.

The killing, Fargo realized, would have to be reserved for Devil's Den if possible. It wasn't just Fargo who might end up in a hemp necktie—the locals could turn on the sheriff, too, for not controlling Fargo.

But at least, the Trailsman resolved, he could remind this bunch of smug, toothless bastards that turnabout was fair play.

Fargo had drawn a day's wages right before he left for town. He ordered a beer and sipped it, biding his time. When he was certain Stan and Sebastian were well on their way back, he drained his mug.

"Well, Silas," he called out, clapping his hat on, "keep your short leg warm, buddy."

"Play it smart, Fargo," Silas muttered. "All five are about to swarm."

Fargo got out of the saloon and into the saddle with quick precision, thumping the Ovaro's flanks as he ki-yied him out to a run. Before he even broke the town limits Fargo had his chin in the mane and the devil on his tail.

Fargo now depended, despite his aversion to fast riding after dark, on sheer luck and the Ovaro's speed. He had earlier selected several good spots where strong saplings grew opposite one another across the only road into Busted Flush.

When he estimated he had opened a big enough lead, Fargo hauled back on the reins and then tossed them forward as he leaped down. He grabbed the coil of six-twine rope from his saddle horn and rushed to one of the saplings, securing the rope with a double hitch.

To make this rope trap work, Fargo knew from mixed experience, the rope had to be stretched taut across the road at the perfect height: too low and the horses' hooves would clear it, too high and horse and rider could spot it.

By the time Fargo began securing the rope to the second sapling, he could hear the Scofield boys pounding closer, shouting and whistling. One of them fired a handgun at the moon.

Even closer on a rataplan of rapid, war-drum hooves, punctuated by shrill whistles, mountain yodels, the sharp reports of weapons. And now, with Fargo about to be stampeded and leading the Ovaro into a straggle of pines, the stallion reared up and almost pulled him off his feet.

Fargo could hear the Scofield horses blowing, irons thundering, as they grew perilously close enough to spot Fargo in the generous moonlight.

"Knock off the shit, old campaigner," he coaxed. "They'll blow both of us to trap bait."

The Ovaro whiffled and gave in, surging into the tree cover and following Fargo even farther back. The Scofield brothers were running their horses three abreast at a breakneck pace, Lem and Bubba bringing up close behind.

The sound, when their mounts' feet ran full bore into the taut rope, was like fifty Indians releasing their bowstrings as one. One horse missed the rope, but two more cartwheeled hard to the ground and brought the other two down on top of them.

Horses neighed shrilly, scuffing and scraping noises erupted, and men cursed in anger and pain.

At least one horse had snapped a leg—Fargo had heard a loud sound like green wood cracking. One Scofield boy lay dazed in the road.

"That cockchafer!" shouted a voice Fargo recognized. "That motherfu—"

"Hey, Eb!" Fargo called out. "You still sweet on me? I see you fell for me hard!"

The moment he fell silent Fargo moved to a new position. Only seconds later the outraged Scofield boys opened up blindly in the direction of Fargo's voice. Most of the slugs cut through well to his right.

But then Fargo drew the joker.

Either by instinct or chance, Romer fired one barrel of the scattergun dangerously close to Fargo's position.

Most of the buckshot sprayed harmlessly into the tree cover near Fargo, and some pellets were stopped by trees in front of him. But several tagged him in the thighs and left side like hot nails driving into him.

Fargo flinched hard and inadvertently backed against a bush hard, rustling it.

"I got a bead, boys!" Romer exalted, and Fargo knew he was an eyeblink away from a second, perhaps lethal blast.

Silently cursing his luck, he was forced to jerk blue steel back and squeeze off three shots in rapid succession. He aimed them toward the spot of the Greener's last muzzle flash.

An almost feminine scream rent the dark fabric of the night, raising Fargo's hackles.

"I'm gut shot, boys!" Romer rasped, his voice tight with pain. "He's killed me, boys! Christ, my guts is on fire!"

Again the high-pitched scream of pain that always marked a man with his entrails blown apart. Fargo's hand was forced now. If he didn't seize the moment while the rest of the Scofields were still unnerved by that banshee scream, they would rally and bathe him in hot lead.

Deliberately shooting inches over their heads, he emptied the remaining three chambers and, hands working deftly in the dark, snapped in the spare cylinder, sending six more slugs whistling in.

This was enough to break the back of the attack. They

commandeered their shaken mounts, deserted their dying kin, and fled back toward the safety of town.

Fargo thumbed reloads, moved out into the road and shot the crying horse. He turned his smoking gun on Romer, whose ululating screams were unstringing his nerves.

"It was Eb I wanted," Fargo said. "But you'll do for starters."

He blew Romer's brains out in a spray of pebbly clots.

"Hold still, dammit," Cranky Man complained. "There's only one left."

"Hold still? Hell, you're going at it like a butcher, not a surgeon," Fargo shot back. "I told you to pry them out with the tip of the blade, not cut into me like a side of beef."

"Then you shoulda brought me that bottle I asked for. I do my best doctoring when I'm drunk. There, ball baby, that's the last one."

Cranky Man tossed the shotgun pellet aside. Fargo splashed carbolic on his wounds, then alum powder to stem the oozing blood. Marcella patched them with isinglass plaster.

"Will the Scofields attack us tonight?" she fretted.

"I don't think so," Fargo replied. "The station is surrounded by too much flat, open ground and there's a full moon. And being yellow-dog cowards like most criminals, they don't like the odds in a fair fight."

"Perhaps, but you did kill one of them, after all. I've heard of these Arkansas blood feuds."

"If they gave a damn about their brother, they wouldn't have left him in the road. These are ambush killers working strictly for Deacon's money, not men bound for glory. They *will* retaliate eventually, though."

"What's the difference?" Sebastian said. "They're making our life miserable anyhow. Might's well even the slate a little."

Marcella, Malinda, Dagobert, Stan, Sebastian and Cecil had crowded around Fargo in the hay barn. Jeremiah Pullman, toting a long Jennings rifle, was on guard out in the yard.

"We heard the shooting earlier," Stan told Fargo. "Sounded like it would never stop. I figured you were celestial by now, Skye."

"I jumped over a snake that time," Fargo agreed. "But I

was hoping to avoid any killing that close to Busted Flush. Now it's done and we can't drag this deal out."

Fargo hadn't pulled his shirt back on yet. Malinda reached out and rubbed a slim white hand across Fargo's muscle-slabbed chest. "My lands, Skye, you certainly are strong."

"Get back to bed," Marcella snapped. "You couldn't be any more obvious if you wore a pinned-up scarlet petticoat."

"Unlike you I don't sleep with my hands outside the blankets, either," Malinda taunted her, flashing an up-and-under look at Fargo before she sashayed out of the barn.

"I believe your sister," remarked Dagobert, who still wore his green eyeshades, "is what is termed a fast young lady."

"Damn you, Fargo," Cranky Man said. "In ten minutes I go on guard. Thank you all to hell and back for waking me up."

"Put away the violin," Fargo said. "I got you out of jail, didn't I? Just make sure you relieve me at midnight and not before. I advise all you folks to turn in. Marcella, do you know how to use this?"

He showed her Romer's Greener.

"Yes. My father taught both of us girls how to use a shotgun."

"Good. Keep it with you tonight just in case. In fact, keep it handy at all times. And anytime you have to take the buckboard into Busted Flush, make sure it's with you. Better yet, you girls shouldn't go alone."

Fargo washed up quickly at the pump in the yard. He noticed that Jeremiah Pullman, despite all his earlier complaining, was remaining vigilant as he patrolled the Ozark West property.

Fargo turned in shortly after ten p.m. and fell asleep almost as soon as his head hit the pillow. He was instantly awake, however, the moment he heard his door meowing slowly open.

He reached behind him to the bedpost and slid his Colt from its holster, thumb-cocking the hammer. The sound was loud in the stillness of the room.

"Please don't shoot me, Skye," came an urgent whisper. "It's Malinda. May I come in?"

"Happy to have your company," Fargo assured her, sitting up in bed and grinning like a butcher's dog.

She entered the room, carrying a two-branch candelabra.

She wore only a chemise, her auburn hair loose and water-falling over her slim shoulders.

"Well, now," Fargo said as she set the candles on the high-boy, "having trouble sleeping?"

"Sort of. You see, I've been touching myself and thinking about you," she replied boldly.

"Oh? Touching yourself where?"

"In my girl place, silly. Where else?"

"Nothing wrong with that," Fargo assured her, feeling his manhood rapidly uncoil and come to rigid attention.

She sat on the very edge of the mattress. "Do you touch yourself, Skye?"

"Sure, but it's not my first choice," he hinted. "Why'n't you lie down here beside me and we'll touch each other."

"Well . . ." She trailed coyly off. "Skye, am I the kind of girl you'd like to do the 'f' word to?"

Fargo fought back a grin. Marcella was sure right: her little sister was a cock tease. Just hearing a young woman say "the 'f' word" made belly flies stir.

"*Just* the kind of girl," he assured her. "Long as we're both here, why don't we?"

"Well . . . maybe it would be all right if you just suck my boobies. But that's *all*."

She pulled the chemise up around her neck and lay back on the bed, an ivory carving of seductive beauty in the flat-tering candlelight. Her tits were luscious mounds like ice cream topped with cherries, her stomach taut and flawless, the V of mons hair silken and shiny.

"Am I nice?" she goaded him in a husky whisper.

"Oh, you're high-grade, all right," Fargo assured her, low-ering his mouth onto one of her luscious tits.

He felt her shudder as he worked her with lips, tongue and teeth, sucking, licking, taking little fish nibbles that made her gasp repeatedly. By now Fargo's man gland was pound-ing with hot blood. He rolled close enough to let her feel the pulsating furrow pressing into her.

"My goodness!" she exclaimed with feigned naïveté. "Have I aroused you?"

"You might say there's a bone of contention between us," Fargo quipped.

She gingerly touched the swollen bulge with exploring fingers. "My, you have a *huge* tallywhacker! Did I really do that to you, Skye?"

"It wasn't the butter-and-egg man, darlin'."

"Oh, then we've gone too far! Please don't ravage me!"

Despite his demanding lust, Fargo had to bite his lip to keep from laughing outright. This little tease was an operator, all right. She slid quickly out of bed and Fargo made a grab for her.

She pirouetted out of his reach, laughing gaily as she picked up the candelabra. "I better go before we start something I can't stop."

"You mean I'm going to have to do the laundry by hand tonight?"

"Naughty man! Think about me while you do it. Think about doing the 'f' word to me."

"I will," Fargo promised, and to taunt her right back he added: "Last night I thought about Marcella while I did it. I worked it for an hour."

She stopped halfway to the door and whirled around. The breathy coyness deserted her voice, replaced by irritation.

"Marcella! *She* won't give it up. She's as cold as last night's mashed potatoes."

"Oh, I think I can warm those taters."

"And to think I let you suck my boobies!"

She flounced out in a huff and Fargo laughed in the dark. Some men would have been enraged—even driven to rape— by a woman who let them go that far before cutting off the sugar. Fargo, however, who sometimes got bored by easy conquests, found this tease game as entertaining as a bull-and-bear match.

Maybe neither one of these lovely sisters fully realized it yet, but randy stallion Skye Fargo was going to screw both of them until hell wouldn't have it again.

Fargo started violently when Cranky Man's mirthless laugh erupted outside the open window.

"Tough luck, Trailsman. You'll have to put off doing the laundry for now. It's two o'clock."

9

At first Fargo's killing of Romer Scofield bought a respite in the violence against Ozark West Transfer Line's main station outside Busted Flush.

Two days passed without incident. Nor were freight or mail runs impeded.

"Sir," "Professor" Dagobert Hastings announced at breakfast on the fifth morning since Marcella Scott had hired Fargo, "you have given us succor."

Fargo's eyes narrowed. "Succor? I don't much like the sound of that."

"It simply means relief."

"Then why not just *say* relief? Anyhow, don't tack up bunting just yet. I'll guarandamntee the worst is yet to come."

And in fact, although Fargo had not mentioned it, the seeming peace had been broken one day earlier only fifteen miles to the south in the outlaw haven of Devil's Den.

Fargo and Cranky Man had ridden there for an extended scout of this region so favored by the Scofield boys, a startling expanse of ravines, crevices, fracture caves and mountain bluff overlooks as far as the eye could see.

Fargo possessed a set of U.S. Army topographical maps and had studied the Northwest Arkansas sector minutely. Devil's Den, in the Boston Mountain subrange, was part of the southernmost, highest and most heavily eroded of the trio of vast plateaus that had created the Ozark Mountains.

A huge creek that often flooded ran through the heart of it and over aeons had sliced through striations of shale, limestone and sandstone, exposing them to view and giving the terrain a unique look found nowhere else in the Ozark region.

"Christ," Cranky Man said as the two men surveyed it from a high bluff, "it looks like some pissed-off giant stomped all over the hills."

Fargo had to agree. It was easy to see that a huge swath of the hills had collapsed into the creek valley beneath them, fracturing huge blocks of sandstone and forming caves and crevices—scores of caves favored by desperate owl hoots on the prod. One of them, Devil's Den Cave, was said to stretch 550 feet into the hillside.

"Look," Fargo said, pointing.

Far below, a Butterfield stagecoach rolled toward its relay station at West Fork, the terminus for the Ozark West mail run.

"Picking up the mail," Fargo said. "And there's an express guard on the box with the driver and another on the roof of the coach. Tells you something about the danger in these parts."

"Yeah. But the Ozark West line don't have any," Cranky Man pointed out. "No wonder drivers are quitting."

"I told Marcella she needs one for each run. She agrees, but until Anslowe Deacon stops gumming up the works for her she hasn't got the money."

"You should have killed him when you had him under the gun. You do that all the time—you let some bottom-feeding piece of shit go when you know that killing him would save a world of misery."

"Sure," Fargo retorted, "just like in them cheap nickel novels you can't read, huh? And if I had blown his lamp out, I'd be holed up right now in one of those caves down there until bloodhounds sniffed me out."

"So what? Way you're going, you'll end up in one anyhow."

Fargo began his scout by riding the elevated perimeter of Devil's Den, especially noting the trails the Scofield boys might use after attacking mail coaches or freight wagons on the road below. Knowing they might be watching him even now, he stuck to the widespread tree cover as much as possible.

Waterfalls were plentiful, as were eerily shaped, wind-sculpted rock formations that local Indians had once named and left gifts to. After several hours in the higher reaches they descended into the valley, crossing a log-and-stone bridge over the frothing creek. Water-rounded stones dotted the bed.

They rode past beautiful Mountain Lake and stopped to water the horses. Fargo had once camped on its shores in late fall. The dazzling colors of change of season had kept him around for an extra two days. But the peaceful beauty had not deceived him—the surrounding hills had been crawling with outlaw gangs.

Fargo's voice interrupted the silence. "Somebody's watching us."

Cranky Man pulled the clay pipe from his mouth. "Where is he?"

"I ain't got the foggiest notion in hell. But my stallion is picking up a human scent—he keeps pricking his ears toward the bluffs to the south."

"There're a few people living in this area," Cranky Man reminded him. "Don't mean somebody's watching us."

"I'm not in the habit of assuming the best."

They forked leather and Fargo led the way toward the area of sandstone crevices and fracture caves.

Cranky Man recalled something and snorted. "I was hiding from the law one time after I jumped the rez and stole this horse. I made the mistake of picking Big Ear Cave to hide in."

Fargo's lips twitched into a grin. That cave was named for the Ozark big-eared bats that hibernated there by the thousands. "They attack you?"

"Nah. But I woke up covered in bat shit."

As the Ovaro walked, Fargo leaned low out of the saddle, studying sign. There were tracks made by horses and men, but none very recently.

Until they rode near the entrance of Devil's Den Cave.

Fargo swung down and studied the prints.

"The edges are just starting to crumble on the newest ones," he said. "One horse and rider stopped here no more than two days ago."

He studied the prints a few minutes longer. "The same horse and the same rider. He's been coming here alone for quite a while. And the boot prints go in and out of the cave."

He glanced into the cave. The fracture caves had been

formed by crumbling blocks of sandstone, and shafts of light speared through the cracks between fragments.

"I'll take a quick squint around inside," he told Cranky Man. "Stay here with the horses and keep your eyes skinned."

Fargo had taken only three strides toward the entrance before dirt suddenly plumed up near his right boot. A fractional second later the crack of a high-power rifle boomed in retreating echoes through the surrounding hills.

Both men dove behind chunks of broken sandstone. A second slug punched into Fargo's stone and pulverized a corner of it.

"Can you spot him?" Cranky Man asked.

"He's too far up there in the trees. Judging from the time between the impact of the slugs and the sound of the weapon firing, he's at least seven hundred yards out. Maybe more."

A third slug chunked into the sandstone protecting Fargo.

"Don't that sound like a Big Fifty?" Cranky Man called over to him.

"Sure's hell does. Hits like one, too. I'd say there's something inside that cave that Eb Scofield doesn't want us to see."

The horses, at least, were safe. The men had hobbled them behind a big pile of scree.

"Fargo, can you get at him with the Henry?"

"It's a forlorn hope," Fargo replied. "And a waste of ammo. My rifle shells got only a little more than a third of the powder grains in a Big Fifty cartridge. 'Sides, I can't even spot any powder haze that far up. Trees are holding it down."

They waited, but there were no more shots. At Fargo's signal both men broke toward their hidden mounts.

"He's got a clear shot at that cave," Fargo said, loosening the Ovaro's hobbles. "And there's too much daylight left to wait him out. And if we do wait, how will we see in there after dark? Let's just pound leather. We'll come back some night with torches."

"I wish I was back in jail," Cranky Man complained. "Least I was safe there."

But a moment later he added: "What the hell could be in that cave? Stolen loot?"

"Hell, how would I know? I got no crystal ball. Maybe nothing. Could be that I just gave him a good target when I was closer to the entrance. Now put a tether on your tongue and get horsed."

Another peaceful day had passed at the Busted Flush station since the shooting incident at Devil's Den. But Fargo, feeling imminent trouble was afoot, had put a pin in the idea of returning to the cave and instead spent each night at the station house.

Fargo had not forgotten Marcella Scott's fear that someone employed at Ozark West had either stolen that expensive emerald-and-diamond bracelet or provided information to whoever did. He observed everyone closely, even Cecil and Malinda.

Breakfast and supper were the only occasions when the men were together as a group. Stan McKinney and Sebastian Kilroy had taken an instant liking to Fargo, and he to them. But he cautioned himself to remember that a man working secretly for Anslowe Deacon might well use affability as a smoke screen.

Lonny Munro, the blacksmith and wheelwright who rarely smiled or spoke to anyone, was a hard worker who was indifferent but not hostile. If he was secretly on Deacon's payroll, he sure's hell wasn't covering the fact with a facade of cheerful friendliness.

Jeremiah Pullman was always shooting off his chin with complaints, but Fargo had to admit he wasn't a shirker. Besides, he was a new hire and wasn't around when that bracelet was stolen.

As for Cecil, Fargo found it hard to believe that a twelve-year-old kid, especially a boy who aspired to be a Texas Ranger, would give a damn about Truella Brubaker's bracelet—nor did he spend much time in the house, outside of meals.

Malinda clearly resented and disliked her sister. But Marcella's court date was now only eleven days away, and what would Malinda do if Marcella was sent to a woman's penitentiary? She clearly had no interest in running a short-line transfer.

Then again, Fargo reminded himself, she just as clearly didn't like Arkansas. He had heard her mention several times that she missed Ohio. With Marcella locked up, Malinda was free to sell Ozark West and return to her home state.

And then there was Dagobert Hastings . . .

Fargo didn't particularly like the annoying, pontificating pedant, but he, too, was a tireless worker who seemed devoted to both the dead Orrin Scott and his pretty niece Marcella. Fargo also agreed that Dagobert hardly seemed the money-grubbing type. When his nose wasn't stuck in the accounts ledger, it was pressed into a volume of Shakespeare, Homer or Plato.

Above all else, however, was the very real possibility—perhaps even probability—that no one at Ozark West was a traitor to the company.

"Here's a lulu for you, gents," Sebastian Kilroy said at the supper table on Fargo's fifth night at the station. "It's Sunday and this gospel shouter is wound up to a fare-thee-well. 'Everything God made is perfect!' he shouts to the audience.

"Well, this hunchback stands up at the back of the revival tent. 'What about me?' he shouts back.

"'Brother,' says the preacher, 'you are the most perfect hunchback I ever saw.'"

Fargo joined in the general laughter, even Lonny Munro cracking a brief grin.

"Quite amusing," Dagobert allowed. "And like many jokes it actually contains a nugget of profound truth about the hypocrisies men live by."

"And here I just thought it was funny," Fargo said.

Dagobert fixed his myopic attention on Fargo, who was rapidly demolishing a delicious hunk of blackberry cobbler.

"Mr. Fargo," he said, "I generally admire the 'frontier type.' But a harsh land produces harsh men who suffer from a paralysis of the inventive faculties."

"That's way too far north for me, Professor. Is all that fancy language your way of insulting me without risk of getting busted in the chops?"

"Of course not. But, for example, in all your wide travels have you ever written—or even read—a poem?"

"I know some dirty rhymes and a few snatches from Longfellow and that crowd. I admit I couldn't last one day in a college. But you wouldn't last one day in Utah's Salt Desert, either, or survive a winter blizzard in the Bitterroot Mountains."

"Touché," Dagobert said.

Fargo took a plate out to Cranky Man in the hay barn.

"Keep your nose in the wind," Fargo warned. "It's been two days since I doused Romer Scofield's glims, and by now those crackers are ready to hit back somehow."

"How do I always get sucked into this shit?" Cranky Man complained. "The white man wouldn't piss in my ear if my brains was on fire. Yet here I am again, exposed like a set of dog balls in a paleface battle."

"Red man's burden," Fargo said solemnly. "Red man's burden."

"Kiss my ass, Fargo."

Cranky Man sat in the straw and seemed to inhale his supper. Afterward, he took out his clay pipe and a pouch of his version of kinnikinnick, a mixture of white man's tobacco and the dried inner bark of the red willow. Fargo liked the sweet smell of it and it kept mosquitoes off.

"Be careful smoking in this barn," Fargo admonished him. "All this hay and straw could go up just like"—Fargo snapped his fingers—"*that.*"

"Get off my dick," the Choctaw snapped. "Go play hide the sausage with Malinda and leave me alone."

Fargo did indeed hope the little tease would show up that night, but at first it didn't seem likely.

Cranky Man woke him at midnight for his two hours of yard-sentry duty, which proved uneventful. At two a.m. Fargo woke up Sebastian and gave him the timepiece, returning to bed.

A soft tapping at the door woke Fargo up, hopeful and smiling.

"Skye," Malinda whispered, "may I come in?"

Fargo opened his mouth to reply in the affirmative. Just then he glanced at the window and felt his scalp tighten.

A lurid, yellow-orange glow had replaced the darkness.

"Fire!" a man's scared voice bellowed from outside. "Everybody up and on the line! *Fire!* The hay barn is burning and Cecil and the Indian are trapped inside!"

10

Fargo didn't waste time running through the house—he stabbed his feet into his boots and vaulted over the windowsill.

Cranky Man and that goddamn pipe, he thought as he raced around the back corner of the station house. And the Ovaro, too, was trapped in that barn . . .

At Fargo's first glimpse of the burning structure a ball of ice replaced his stomach. The barn was a raging inferno, all those stacks of hay fueling tongues of flame that leaped and danced high into the night sky with a flapping, roaring sound.

Night had been turned into day, and furnace heat radiated in all directions. Fargo found Stan McKinney valiantly trying to charge into the barn, but being driven back each time.

"It started in the back!" he told Fargo, his voice raised above the crackling roar of the flames. "I saw it out my window. I'm trying to at least lead the horses out! I don't see Cecil or Cranky Man anywhere."

It started in the back, Fargo thought. Then Cranky Man didn't likely start it. His stall was way up front.

There were about a dozen horses inside the barn, and Fargo could hear them neighing in abject terror and wildly kicking at their stalls. Dagobert, Jeremiah Pullman and Lonny Munro joined them, followed by Marcella and Malinda.

"Dagobert, Munro!" Fargo shouted. "That house has a shake roof and there're embers flying onto it. Grab a ladder and shovels and get on top of the house. Smother those embers!"

"Look!" Stan shouted. "I'll be damned!"

The Ovaro and Cranky Man's skewbald, then more of the horses, bolted in a panic from the barn.

"Hee-*yah*!" Cranky Man's voice shouted from inside, followed by sharp whistles and whoops. "Hee-*yah*!"

"The Choctaw is driving them out!" Stan said. "That gutsy son of a buck had best get out himself 'fore the whole thing collapses!"

As if to underscore Stan's warning, a huge section of the barn roof suddenly collapsed in a crash of burning timbers, showering those in the yard with sparks.

Fargo immersed himself in the stone water trough, then pulled his bandanna up over his nose and mouth.

"It's too dang hot, Fargo!" Stan warned. "You'll never get inside!"

Fargo ignored him and hurled himself toward the fiery hell, counting on speed and momentum to propel him if courage gave out.

The blistering heat was like being immersed in a giant cauldron of scalding water, and it felt as if every nerve ending in his body had been stripped raw for maximum pain.

Somehow Fargo pushed through the burning doors into a tunnel of billowing, acrid smoke. Only a few feet inside the door he tripped over a body. It was Cranky Man, and Cecil was in his arms. They were both either dead or overcome by smoke—just as a choking, coughing Fargo was about to be as the fire sucked up all the oxygen.

Fargo's wet buckskins were steaming. Another section of the burning roof collapsed, falling timbers barely missing him.

Summoning reserves of strength and endurance he didn't know he possessed, Fargo grabbed Cranky Man by one ankle, Cecil by another, and managed to drag them outside before he collapsed.

Pullman, Stan and Munro dashed forward and dragged all three farther out of harm's way even as the entire barn suddenly caved in on itself in a roaring crash and giant tower of sparks.

Blessed coolness washed over Fargo as the two sisters frantically began dousing the three of them with pails of water. All three began to revive.

"That crazy, cantankerous Choctaw," Fargo said as he sat up, "is a damn hero. He drove the horses out and then went back into the guts of the fire and got the kid. If he hadn't carried him so close to the doors, I never could have grabbed Cecil."

"You heard the man," Cranky Man said hoarsely, struggling up on one elbow. "I want a bottle—I earned it."

Dagobert and Munro were succeeding atop the station house, tamping out the embers before they could start blazes.

"By the lord Harry!" Stan swore. "There goes our barn and all our hay. We're up the creek without a paddle now."

"I'll bet that stinking Indian started it on purpose," Malinda said. "He's a sneaky, hateful savage."

"If so, genius," Marcella snapped, "why did Mr. Fargo have to drag him to safety?"

"Well, then maybe he started it through carelessness or stupidity."

"Say," Fargo interrupted the brewing catfight, "where's Sebastian? He's s'posed to be walking guard and I haven't seen him once."

This initiated a quick search.

"Over here by the corral!" Pullman called out. "He's alive, but looks like he was hit hard on the head."

Sebastian, moaning and not quite conscious, lay sprawled in the dirt, blood clotting the hair on his pate. Lonny Munro ran for water to revive him.

"Well, unless Cranky Man also conked Sebastian on the cabeza," Fargo said, "this clears him."

Cecil coughed a few times to find his voice. "I didn't start no fire," he protested. "I was fast asleep. So was Cranky Man. I 'member him snoring real loud."

"It's a mortal shame," Stan lamented. "With that hay gone, we're nigh at the end of our string."

"It was the Scofields," Marcella announced with finality. "Revenge for the killing of their kin. I knew they'd strike back."

"Distinct possibility," Fargo said. "But do you remember that little talk we had in your office about the drawer?"

Her startled eyes met Fargo's, coruscating in the reflection from the dying flames. She hadn't thought about the possibility of inside sabotage.

She said, "You don't mean . . . ?"

"I don't know what I mean," Fargo replied. "But don't stack your conclusions higher than your evidence. Wait till Sebastian comes around and we talk to him. And I'll know more come sunup when I can take a good look around the yard."

Sebastian Kilroy was in no shape to answer questions right away. The men carried him to his bed and Marcella washed his wound before he drifted into sleep.

Now that Cranky Man was a hero of sorts, Marcella insisted on making sleeping pallets for him and the likewise displaced Cecil in a lean-to built off the back of the station house. Fargo turned in for the few remaining hours until sunrise.

When the light was sufficient, about an hour after sunup, Fargo began the laborious task of trying to find sign in the big yard. Stan McKinney had already hitched two teams into harness, one for Sebastian Kilroy's Concord mail-run coach, the other for Jeremiah Pullman's big Owensboro freight wagon.

With Sebastian laid up, and the mail run imperative, Lonny Munro had volunteered to whip the stage between Fayetteville and West Fork.

"See anything yet?" Stan asked as he joined Fargo near the corral where Sebastian had been found.

"That's just the trouble," Fargo replied. "There's too damn much to see."

Fargo rose from a deep squat to stretch the kinks from his back.

"The yard, especially right around here," he added, "is too crowded with prints: boot prints, animal prints, wagon tracks. I should've told you to send the teams out in a different direction this morning. They both rolled right over this spot."

"More of my damn stupidity," Stan apologized. "I don't think like a trailsman."

"Ain't your fault, Stan. You were busy doing your job."

Fargo glanced toward the house. He was thinking out loud more than speaking with his next remark.

"I can't even tell if anybody came from the station. Sometimes you can tell fresh prints from the bend of the grass. But with the fire last night, and a bunch of us running all over, it's no use."

"If anybody came from the station?" Stan repeated in a surprised tone. "Do you mean you think one of *us* attacked Sebastian?"

Open mouth, insert foot, Fargo chastised himself. The last thing he wanted was to tip off the workers that they were under possible suspicion.

"Of course not," Fargo scoffed. "I just meant that an intruder might've come from that direction. You know, maybe hiding behind the house."

"Oh. So you think whoever it was came in on foot?"

"I sure would if I was a barn burner. It's quieter and a horse is mighty hard to hide. But I wouldn't have my horse too far away. So now I'm going to take a look-see farther out."

"Jiminy, Fargo, are you sure that's wise? They've already tried to plug you from the hills. If somebody's out there now—"

"Believe me," Fargo cut him off, "that thought has crossed my mind a few hundred times."

"Is it really that important," Stan pressed him, gazing toward the still-smoking heap that had once been the barn, "to find tracks? I mean, seems to me we know who fired up that barn. Why risk your hide proving that water is wet?"

Fargo couldn't tell him the truth: that he was really trying to make sure there *had been* an outside intruder. He liked Stan and felt like a weasel.

"Remember," Fargo said, "we don't really know for certain-sure that fire was set deliberately. It's best to confirm it."

"What? But Sebastian was knocked out cold. Don't that confirm it?"

"It does for me," Fargo floundered, "but I like all the proof I can get before I start peddling lead."

This was weak, and Stan gave him a curious look. But he was too polite to challenge Fargo.

"Yeah, I reckon that's so," he said without conviction. "But accident or no, this is a helluva setback. Hay ain't a big crop in these parts, and most of ours was shipped alla way from Jonesboro at a mighty steep lay. It'll take weeks to get more. And with profits way down, thanks to Deacon, I ain't so sure Marcella can afford a big shipment right now."

"Maybe we can do something about that," Fargo remarked without elaborating. "I see there's a small granary behind the smithy?"

"Well, we got a couple dozen barrels of crushed barley and parched corn that's mostly meant for the horses. I'll have to feed it to the mules now, but it can't hold out more than a week or so."

Cranky Man joined them with Cecil dogging his heels.

"Fargo, get this kid off my ass, wouldja?" the Choctaw complained. "Hell, he's took to following me like a pet."

Fargo forced back a grin. "Well, sure, noble red man. You saved his life."

"Like hell I did! I was just using him as a shield to keep the flames off me."

"Nuh-unh," Cecil said. "You was sleeping right up front by the doors. You had to come halfways back into the barn to get me."

"Kid, you're nothing but a burr in my blanket," Cranky Man groused. "Why'n't you go count your toes or something?"

Half expecting a gunshot from the hills at any moment, Fargo walked out past the wagon yard to the ground surrounding Ozark West property. For well over an hour he patiently circled the perimeter, eyes scouring the ground. It was mostly grass with patches of sand, but he found no sign of fresh prints.

However, there was a long rock spine at one point leading almost up to the yard. A man could walk a horse in quietly and then cross a short expanse of grass to the barn. The wind had whipped around furiously earlier this morning, lifting and waving the grass and possibly destroying any bend in it left by a man.

By the time Fargo returned to the house Sebastian was awake and sitting up in bed, looking pale and eating a bowl of grits. Marcella sat in a chair beside the bed.

"Did you find out anything?" Marcella asked the Trailsman.

"Not much," Fargo replied, sending her a look that said *we'll talk later.*

He looked at Sebastian. "How you feeling, old son?"

"Like drunk Pawnees been using my head for a war drum."

"You got any idea who hit you?"

"I don't, Skye, consarn it. I was having a smoke and watching out toward the hills. I was trying to figure out if there was a horse out on the flat, you know, just standing with its head down."

"You think there was?"

"I was trying to see, but this big raft of clouds blew over the moon, and it was all slippery shadows out there. One second I thought I seen it, and then the next I wasn't sure. Anyhow, I heard something behind me and then, next rattle out of the box, I was hearing angels."

Fargo nodded. "Well, rest up. Maybe something will come to you later."

He flashed Marcella a signal with his eyes and they moved out into the hallway.

"What is it?" she asked anxiously.

"Marcella, I tend to agree with you: somebody around here *might* be sailing under false colors."

"So you did find something out there?"

"I tried but came up with nothing but the sniffles. A better tracker than me might be able to say for sure."

"From what I hear, there *is* no better tracker than you."

"You hear wrong, lady. I rate high among white trackers, but Indians are the best."

"Well, your friend Cranky Man is an Indian."

Fargo gave her a rueful grin. "Cranky Man has his useful qualities. And as you saw last night, he's fearless when the chips are down. But he's lazy when it comes to hard work, and tracking is hard work. I doubt if he could follow a herd of buffalo in fresh snow."

Her face collapsed into a study in hopeless misery. "What are we going to do?"

"Look at it this way: one way or another Deacon is behind what happened last night. And it's Deacon who's going to answer for it."

"What is your plan?"

"Right now," Fargo said, "it's just scratched out in the dirt. And the less you know, the better. But I'm going to do it pretty pronto. Deacon's going to get the message loud and clear that every strike will be answered."

"I know your reasoning is sound, but I'm scared."

"Yeah, but you're a strong woman. This is war, Marcella, and you've got to destroy your enemy before he can destroy you."

11

The four surviving members of the Scofield boys were half-way through a jug of mountain lightning, and homicide glinted in their eyes.

"Won't be long, boys," announced Stanton Scofield, "and Skye Goddamn Fargo will be taking the Big Jump. You don't kill a Scofield and then ride off like it's none of your beeswax."

"Maybe so, but you boys oughta got your brother's body sooner," said Cousin Lem the arsonist. "The carrion birds et his damn eyeballs out. It give me the fantods when I seen that."

Stanton ignored the remark. Lem was a mouthy little shit in need of a good ass-whupping. But his half-wit brother Bubba protected him fiercely, and Bubba was big enough to fight cougars with a shoe.

Eb Scofield stood hip-cocked in the doorway of the cabin, keeping watch up the holler.

"Is the squaw man coming yet?" Stanton asked.

Eb shook his head. "Mayhap the sachet kitten is still soakin' in his fancy French bubble bath."

"I hear that little sissy-bitch takes him two baths a week," Lem said.

"Well, he's fartin' blood now. I'll tell you that," Stanton said. "Fargo tricked Deacon's Cherokee whore into killing one of his workers, and Fargo crippled up another. When he gets here, ol' Deacon's gonna ream us a new one on account Fargo ain't dead yet. Let him blow off steam, boys. I like the wages just fine."

"He oughta be happy 'bout the barn fire," Eb pointed out. "Lem done fine work there."

"I had good help puttin' that sentry out," Lem said.

"Well, we *best* kill Fargo in a puffin' hurry," Eb added. "The son of a bitch is pokin' around Devil's Den Cave."

"Why are you watching that cave so damn close?" Stanton demanded. "It's just a itty-bitty bracelet, and you said you hid it real good. Hell, Fargo won't find it in a cave that big."

Eb averted his eyes. "I just don't like him snooping around there, 'at's all."

"Horseshit! You stole somethin' else and hid it there, di'n't ya? That's how's come you're alla time saying you know some secret about Marcella Scott and what a filthy Jezebel she is."

Soft singing interrupted the conversation:

Rockabye, baby, on the treetop,
When the bough breaks the cradle will rock . . .

"Christ Almighty!" Stanton swore under his breath.

His cousin Bubba Scofield sat at the crude deal table, rocking his huge body back and forth and singing softly to the fat black rat cradled against his chest. It was enough to curl the hair on an eggplant.

"Lem," Stanton said in a low voice, "ain't you had a talk with Bubba 'bout that fuckin' rat? Bubba always obeys you."

"It don't do no good this time," Lem replied. "He's jo-fired in love with it. And don't call it a rat so's he can hear you—he's named it Jimmy and treats it like his boy child."

"Here comes the squaw man," Eb announced from the doorway, "all togged out in fancy feathers."

"Christ!" Stanton said. "I can already whiff that stink water he splashes all over him."

Anslowe Deacon pulled rein in front of the cabin and hobbled his horse next to the others. His cruel, long-shanked spurs looked ridiculous buckled over his side-lacing silk riding boots.

He stepped inside the cabin, his piercing black eyes staring at each man in turn.

They widened in disgust when he saw Bubba gently kiss the sewer rat.

"What in pluperfect hell?" he demanded.

"Never mind," Stanton warned. "He's mighty touchy about it."

"You mean he's mighty *touched*."

"Care for a snort?" Lem asked, proffering the jug.

Deacon waved off the offer. "No, thanks. I only drink wine."

"Wine?" Eb scoffed. "Hell, that's just vinegar sneaking up on old age. This shit'll put hair on your pecker."

"Never mind. Let's get down to brass tacks. Why aren't you boys continuing with the harassment of the Ozark West conveyances?"

"Hell," Stanton protested, "we torched the barn last night."

Deacon nodded. "Yes, a job well done and I congratulate you. But I told you it's getting too risky to keep attacking the station. And no more killings except for Fargo, unless you can make absolutely certain they look like natural accidents. There've been two already, and that worthless sheriff in Busted Flush has raised hell about them."

"Gillycuddy?" Lem scoffed. "Hell, he ain't worth a busted trace chain."

"That's beside the mark. He's caught the attention of a crusading ink-slinger in Fayetteville. Tubby Scott was a popular man in these parts. And that driver Eb killed, Miller, has a brother who's a Fayetteville lawman. I can't fend off the pressure forever."

"Jimmy want some din-din?" Bubba's voice interrupted. "Is Jimmy a hungry boy?"

Deacon's fleshy, liver-colored lips twisted in disgust when Bubba began feeding the rat grains of corn.

"You boys didn't tell me he was mad," Deacon complained. "You said he was just slow. I don't want him jeopardizing this mission."

"He ain't no problem," Lem insisted. "He does what he's told."

"There're two goals you need to concentrate on," Deacon reiterated. "First, you need to interrupt the timely flow of mail. Second, you need to kill Fargo, but *not* around here. Do it down in Devil's Den, where it won't be so easy to link my name to it—or yours, for that matter."

"We don't give a frog's fat ass," Stanton retorted, "if our name is linked to it. That son of a bitch killed Romer."

" 'At's right," Eb threw in. "And in these here hills, clans are expected to square accounts when their kin is kilt by outsiders."

Deacon shook his head. "Look, boys, this has got to be done carefully. What your neighbors think or approve isn't the point. You boys can't read, so you've no real idea that Fargo is a newspaper hero. His death will be a big event, and newspaper scribblers will be all over it like dark on night. They'll start turning over stones to expose the slugs clinging beneath."

"Hunh?" Eb said.

Deacon expelled a long, fluming sigh.

"I mean that *all* of our names could be linked to it and there could be a backlash that sinks us. Lure him into Devil's Den by harassing the Ozark West mail coach. And after you kill him, make sure his body will never be found. Unless you kill him I'll never get that mail contract—and if I do, that means a fat bonus for all of you."

"What about the bitch?" Stanton said. "She's facing a judge and jury on account of that fancy bracelet Eb snatched. You yourself said that if she's found guilty, she can't pass the transfer company on. Her sister owns it lock, stock and barrel."

"Yeah," Eb said, "and that sister of her'n don't know her ass from her elbow 'bout running it. 'Sides, Butterfield won't make medicine with a company tarred for thievin'."

"All that might be true," Deacon conceded. "But *only* if Marcella Scott is found guilty."

"What about this fat bitch what owns the bracelet? I heerd she's got a rich husband who's a big nabob in the steamboat business."

"Yes, Truella Brubaker is wealthy and right now it looks bad for Marcella. It doesn't help her cause that she's also an outsider from Ohio who puts on airs. But she's a woman, and pretty, and it's going to be all men on the jury."

"Sure, and what red-blooded man wouldn't ache to poke her," Stanton said. "Hell, I'd give a purty just to sniff her frilly drawers."

"She's a filthy whore and hellfire is too damn good for her," Eb interjected. "I got—"

He suddenly fell silent.

"You got what, brother?" Stanton demanded.

"I know all about her, that's all," Eb said.

Deacon, visibly distracted and worried, ignored all this.

"Besides," he went on, "whether or not she's prosecuted, Fargo isn't going anywhere. The man is implacable. I looked into his eyes and I could see it. Once men attempt to kill him, he'll hang on like a tick until he avenges it."

"Don't you fret about Fargo," Stanton vowed. "We'll trick him into Devil's Den, all right, and leave him cold as a wagon wheel. Won't nobody find his body, neither. And I already got a crackerjack plan for that mail coach."

12

On the night after the hay barn was set ablaze, Fargo took Stan McKinney and Sebastian Kilroy aside after supper.

"Boys," he said as he closed the door of his room, "it's come down to the nut cuttin'. You both know that Ozark West needs fodder to keep those mules in the traces. And you also know who's responsible for that barn fire."

"Ain't no big mystery there," Stan said. "Anslowe Deacon."

"Sure as cats fighting," Sebastian agreed. "Elsewise I wouldn't a spent half the day in bed with my head throbbing."

"You feeling better now?"

"I'll be back on the trail tomorrow."

"All right then," Fargo said. "We can stand around with our thumbs up our sitters or we can replace at least some of that hay. And it's stacked up less than three miles away."

"Deacon's station?" Stan said.

"Who else should post the pony?"

Stan and Sebastian exchanged an uncertain glance in the lamplight.

"Well, he owes it to us, right enough," Stan said. "But you mean . . . just steal it?"

Fargo laughed. "You think I'm gonna *ask* him for it? Hell yes, I mean steal it . . . except it *ain't* stealing—it's owed to Marcella. And after I load it up I'm burning his barn down."

"Holy Hannah!" Sebastian exclaimed. "Skye, they'll come down on us like all wrath! Ozark West is the first bunch they'll blame. 'Sides, Deacon keeps a well-armed guard on his property after dark. You'll have to kill him if you don't want a witness."

"Oh, there'll be no killing or I'll call it off. And if we play this hand right, Ozark West *won't* be taking the blame. Stan, are you willing to stand a double watch from two a.m. to 6 a.m.? That would be Sebastian's watch and yours."

"Well, sure. But where will Sebastian be?"

"With me and Cranky Man. He'll be driving the freight wagon loaded with hay."

"Now, hold on," Sebastian said. "I ain't eager to spend years in prison."

"The only other experienced driver is Pullman," Fargo pointed out, "and I don't think he'll do it. Lonny Munro could whip the team, I s'pose, but I want an experienced knight of the ribbons in case there's trouble."

"Jesus, Skye, I dunno . . ."

"Look, I can't promise we won't all be arrested, but if it comes to that I'll swear I was driving the wagon. You won't even need to be seen."

"Well . . . if we don't do *some*thing mighty damn quick," Sebastian admitted, "Ozark West is done for, I reckon. Deal me in."

Fargo next spoke briefly with Marcella in her office, requesting two bottles of whiskey from the supply pantry.

"But I already gave Cranky Man one earlier today as his reward for his bravery last night," she protested.

"It's not for him or any of us," Fargo said. "You might say it's a form of taking out insurance."

"Mr. Fargo, I don't understand—"

"And you're not going to. The less you know, the better."

When she hesitated, Fargo took her by both shoulders.

"Look, Marcella, you didn't hire me to do things by halves. Desperate situations call for desperate remedies. But you're already facing legal troubles, and I want this matter kept dark from you. Believe me, Ozark West is far from whipped. Now how 'bout that whiskey?"

She mustered a smile. "Two bottles coming up."

Well after midnight Stan hitched four mules into the harness of an Owensboro wagon. He shook the lines and the wagon rattled into motion, Fargo and Cranky Man flanking him on horseback.

It was a dark, cloudy night with poor illumination—exactly what Fargo wanted.

"Pull your hat down low," Fargo told Sebastian. "The Fort Smith Express yard is right at the end of Commerce Street on the edge of town. When I tell you to, rein off the road and just wait in the shadows until you hear me give you the owl hoot."

The short drive was uneventful and no one passed them on the road. Fayetteville looked empty and dark except for a few coal-oil streetlamps toward the center of town.

"All right, Sebastian," Fargo said when they were about fifty yards away from the big corral in front of Deacon's transfer station. "Pull off under those trees and wait for the signal."

"Damn, my back teeth're chattering," the driver replied. "I'm a dang fraidy-cat."

"Bullshit," Fargo scoffed. "You face danger every day when you whip that mail coach. Just stay frosty."

"I don't give a damn about the danger," Cranky Man complained. "You'll likely get me killed anyway before this deal is over. What steams my beans is them two bottles of firewater I seen you poke into your saddlebag. How come I ain't tasted a drop yet?"

"You guzzled a whole bottle already today," Fargo said, dismounting. "Now light down and hobble your horse next to the wagon."

"Fargo, you son of a bitch," Cranky Man said as he obeyed the order. "I hope you die of the runny shits."

Fargo had already wrapped each bottle of liquor in rawhide. Now he tucked them inside his shirt. The two men started toward Fort Smith Express on foot. Fargo shucked out his Colt and palmed the wheel to check the action.

"Here's the deal," he told the Choctaw. "Stan told me there're roundsmen patrolling the town all night. Keep your ears skinned for 'em. He also thinks there's only one night watchman on Deacon's property. But there might be more since our little visit to his quarters a few days back. *Don't* let anybody sneak up on me—I'm gonna be busy."

Both men stopped in the street in front of the big corral, hunkering in the shadows while Fargo reconnoitered the property. Besides the main office, with Deacon's private quarters at the rear, there was a smithy, stock sheds and six conveyances for hauling freight.

Almost the entire right side of the lot was taken up by a

two-story barn, and even from the street Fargo could whiff the nose-tickling tang of hay and alfalfa.

Stan had already told him that, because this Fort Smith Express station was located right in town, the workers did not live on the property. Fargo soon spotted the orange-glowing tip of a cigarette and the dark form of a man pacing around the property.

"All I can see is one guard," Fargo whispered. "Stay right here and watch the street."

He stayed low and circled the big corral to move up behind the guard. Cat-footing closer, Fargo recognized a double-barreled scattergun dangling in the guard's left hand.

Fargo drew the Arkansas toothpick from its boot sheath and silently closed the gap.

"Christ!" The guard froze like a hound on point when the lethal edge of the blade pressed against his windpipe.

"Shut your cake hole," Fargo muttered from behind him. "You make one squawk and I'll turn your throat into a gulch. Savvy that?"

After a pause: "Looks like you got my dick in the wringer, mister. I savvy."

"Smart man. I'm not here to kill you, but that's up to you. Now toss down that smoke pole."

The guard complied. Fargo used his free hand to pull one of the bottles from behind his shirt. He pulled the cork with his teeth.

"You're gonna have a few drinks on me," Fargo said.

"Like hob I will!"

Fargo pressed his knife tighter, taking care not to cut skin. There could be no marks on the man or the entire plan was worthless.

"Mister, either you drink up pronto or you'll be shoveling coal in hell. I don't chew my cabbage twice. And if you spit it out or spill one drop, I'll start by lopping your nuts off. *Don't* force my hand—right now I'm on the ragged edge."

The guard took the bottle, tilted it back, swallowed several times and lowered it.

"Look, mister, I ain't a drinking man. This stuff has got my belly on fire."

"Take a breath and keep guzzling," Fargo said.

"Hell, mister, I can't just—"

In an eyeblink the tip of the toothpick was pressed tight into the guard's family jewels.

"Drink that bottle dry," Fargo growled, "or I'll cut your ball sac open and geld you."

"Jesus, *don't*!"

In little more than a minute the bottle was empty. This rapid intake of potent mash soon brought the guard to his knees, no fight left in him. Fargo knew he would soon pass out, but he wanted to make sure he was still dead drunk when the alarm was raised.

He pulled out the second bottle. This time the groggy, barely conscious but compliant guard swallowed about a third of the contents as Fargo tipped the bottle for him. The guard toppled into the dirt, still breathing but dead to the world. Any more, Fargo thought, and he'll just be dead.

Suddenly Cranky Man whistled softly from out in the street.

Hoping the darkness would obscure him enough, Fargo snatched up the scattergun and turned his back, pacing toward the office.

"Howzit goin', Lowell?" called the voice of a roundsman from the street. At least Fargo hoped it was a roundsman and not Lowell's relief.

"Boring," Fargo called back.

"That ain't no shit. Say, you got any 'baccy?"

"Fresh out."

"Story of my life. Well, keep your powder dry and your pecker hard."

Fargo let out a sigh of relief as the roundsman moved off. But they'd have to work fast—if that roundsman returned too soon, they'd all be breaking rocks in the hot sun.

He splashed some of the remaining whiskey on Lowell's shirt, then corked the bottle and laid it and the empty nearby. Fargo gave the owl hoot and Sebastian and the freight wagon rattled into the yard.

The three men ducked into the barn and lit one of the lanterns hanging from a crosstree.

"No animals inside," Fargo confirmed. "Sebastian, does Ozark West buy alfalfa hay?"

"Not for a long time now."

"All right, we'll just load the cured grass. Marcella won't have invoices to cover alfalfa."

Cranky Man, busy poking around for whiskey in a back corner, suddenly loosed a whistle.

"Shit, there're at least a hundred gunny sacks of grain back here," he said. "Oats and crushed barley."

"We can cut open the bags when we get back," Sebastian said, "and dump it into the granary." He was already heaving bales of hay into the Owensboro wagon.

"All right, but it has to be the minute you get back," Fargo said. "And then burn the sacks. Leave at least half of it here. We don't want to make it look like anything was stolen.

"That's got it," Fargo said when the wagon was loaded. "You two head back. I'm waiting about a half hour before I torch this barn. It'll look like a familiar story: a man got drunk and was careless with a lantern or cigarette."

"Fargo, are you chewing peyote?" Cranky Man demanded. "That guard will just tell what happened when he sobers up."

"When any man except you takes down that much whiskey that fast, there's a good chance he won't remember what happened. Even if he does, and Deacon believes him, the law likely won't. It's exactly the kind of fantastic lie a guilty man would make up to cover his ass. Now dust, both of you."

While Fargo waited he made sure Lowell was lying far enough from the barn to avoid being caught in the fire or falling debris. With roundsmen on the beat, the alarm would go up fairly quickly and the fire brigade would likely assemble quickly enough to save the other buildings. But the remaining hay and alfalfa were excellent tinder, and the barn would be beyond saving.

When he estimated a half hour had ticked by, Fargo kicked over a burning lantern into a mound of loose hay. He waited long enough to make sure the fire was off to a good start, then sprinted the fifty yards back to the Ovaro.

As he reined the stallion back into the road he glanced toward the Fort Smith Express property.

Sawing flames were already crawling up the exterior walls of the barn.

For a moment Fargo recalled Deacon's warning to him

four days ago: *"If I were you I'd be very careful not to step in something you can't wipe off."*

"I give as good as I get," Fargo muttered to the endless night. "And then I add a little bit extra."

He thumped the Ovaro's ribs and they raced off into the black velvet darkness.

13

By the time Fargo returned, Stan and Sebastian had dumped the barley and oats into the granary and stacked the hay in one of the stock sheds.

"If any law dogs come snooping around asking questions," Fargo told Stan, who was walking guard, "that's the hay we managed to save when the Ozark West barn went up."

"Of course it is," Stan replied with a straight face. "I remember fighting off heat and smoke when we done it."

Fargo stripped the leather from the Ovaro and rubbed him down good. After letting the stallion drink his fill, Fargo turned him out into the corral. It was well after four a.m. when a bone-weary Fargo crept silently through the house into his back bedroom.

He thumb-scratched a lucifer to life and turned up the wick of the lamp, lighting it and watching the light push the shadows back into the corners of the room.

The sudden sound of a nearby voice made him flinch.

"I wondered if you'd ever get here," Malinda pouted. "I even fell asleep waiting for you."

Fargo's jaw slacked open at the erotic splendor revealed in the ruddy lamplight. No chemise this time: the shapely little strumpet lay bare-butt naked atop the counterpane on his bed, posing like a model for a Dutch master.

He took in the pretty, fine-boned face framed by shiny billows of sun-streaked auburn hair; the hard mounds of her tits; the hourglass hips and taut stomach; the slender ivory columns of her shapely legs capped at their apex by that exciting delta of silken mons hair—Fargo had always had a strong fascination with a beautiful woman's belly bush.

He swallowed hard as his manhood instantly uncoiled. "Well, now, what have we here?"

She gave him a teasing laugh and coyly pulled a corner of the counterpane over herself.

"Now don't you dare go ravaging me! I always sleep in the nude, and you caught me completely by surprise."

Fargo laughed and unbuckled his gun belt. "I see. Caught you completely by surprise in my bed."

"Are you complaining?"

Fargo sat on the bed to tug off his boots, then stood back up to drop his buckskin trousers and kick out of them.

Malinda's eyes widened and she rose on one elbow to stare at his curved saber, now leaping up and down like a divining rod gone mad.

"My stars and garters! It looks so big and . . . angry!"

"Oh, he's a friendly cuss," Fargo assured her. "But I figure the tease game is over, lady."

He stretched out in bed beside her. Before she could say another word, his strong hands gripped her slight waist and effortlessly swung her over on top of him. For a gal who didn't want to be "ravaged," she readily scissored her legs wide and eagerly tipped his staff just right so that it slid in to the hilt when he lowered her onto him.

She moaned in abandon, not caring who heard her, her hips gyrating to rub her pearly nubbin against the hardness filling her to capacity. Fargo, too, writhed in ecstasy—it felt like a tight velvet glove moving rapidly up and down his tool, sending hot prickles all the way into his groin.

He pumped for only a short time before the first of several rapid climaxes suddenly washed over her, and Malinda shrieked in an abandonment of pleasure, her cries climbing an octave as each climax topped the one before it. Unable to keep the floodgate closed any longer, Fargo nearly bucked her off with his powerful release.

Malinda collapsed over him, a limp rag doll, panting like a dog in the hot moons.

The bedroom door creaked open.

"Since you're over twenty-one I don't interfere with your shameless whoring, little sister," came Marcella's stern voice

83

from the doorway, "but do you *have* to wake up the entire house? I can hear that Indian laughing all the way back in the lean-to. He does a good imitation of you, by the way."

"It's Skye's fault," Malinda shot back breathlessly. "A woman *can't* be quiet with him. Lord, does he know what he's doing!"

"Get back to your room."

Malinda gave Fargo a final kiss, rolled off the bed, picked her chemise up from the floor and shimmied into it, then flounced past her sister.

Fargo expected Marcella to follow her. But he had made no effort to cover himself, and Marcella was staring at his still completely aroused member.

"Congratulations are in order," she told him sarcastically. "Usually she teases a man for weeks before she finally gives it up. I think I'm looking at the reason why it took you less time."

"I aim to please," Fargo said modestly.

He expected her to leave but still she was looking at his arousal like a bird mesmerized by a snake.

"It sounded to me as if both of you had finished," she said. "But apparently I didn't wait long enough for you. I apologize."

"Oh, I finished—with the first time around. It generally takes at least two before J. Henry calms down."

"At *least* two?" she repeated, wonder in her tone.

When she still seemed unable to tear herself away from the door, Fargo said:

"Why'n't you come on in? I'm sure we'd both enjoy it."

She slowly shook her head. "I have to agree, but I don't take my sister's leavings. Good night, Mr. Fargo."

But Fargo had never seen a woman close a door so slowly in his life.

"Sebastian," Fargo said at breakfast later that morning, "after what happened last night, Deacon will have his bristles up. We cost him a lot of kale, and I expect trouble. I'll be riding along with you on the mail run."

"Glad to have the company," Sebastian replied, busy spreading a biscuit with hot bacon grease. "I agree with you about trouble brewing."

"What happened last night," Dagobert spoke up, "that has the two of you fearing retribution?"

Fargo had deliberately kept everyone he could in the dark about Deacon's barn, including the Scott sisters.

"Nothing," Fargo said. "If the law from Fayetteville should come sniffing around, *nothing* is all you know."

Dagobert nodded. "Of course. Men of few words seldom have to take any back. I did notice, however, a goodly amount of hay stacked in one of the stock sheds."

Fargo saw that Cecil was hanging on every word.

"Look, kid," he said, "fix up a plate and take it to Cranky Man."

"Yessir."

"Does that Choctaw," Stan said, "have *any* religion? He swears like a stable sergeant."

"He seems to believe in those magic pebbles of his," Fargo replied. "But he's not a Christian if that's what you mean. He worships whiskey."

Dagobert laid his fork on his plate and assumed his professorial mien.

"Many Indians worship the sun, which white men find foolish," he lectured. "But the ancient Egyptians, too, were sun worshippers and for a very logical reason: they could count on it being there after they were dead. And unlike the abstract Christian God, the sun is something they could *see*."

"You one of them godless heathens?" Jeremiah Pullman snapped.

"Mr. Fargo is."

"Yeah, well, he ain't always shootin' off his mouth about it and selling it to others."

Sebastian, the company peacemaker, changed the subject.

"This woman goes into a gun shop. 'I want to buy a revolver,' she says. 'It's for my husband.' So the gunsmith says, 'Did he tell you what kind to buy?' 'I should say not!' she replies. 'He doesn't even know yet that I'm going to shoot him!' "

Stan cracked up, smacking his thigh, and Fargo mustered a polite smile. Dagobert chuckled, Pullman frowned and the indifferent Lonny Munro simply kept eating as if no one had spoken.

Cecil left with Cranky Man's plate and Dagobert decided to join the levity.

"Gentlemen, I'm reminded of the soiled dove who purchased a book on English grammar. You see, she was ending every sentence with a proposition."

Everybody stared at him blank-faced.

"I don't get it," Fargo said.

Dagobert sighed. "Casting pearls to swine."

On a sudden impulse Fargo said, "Have you ever cast an emerald-and-diamond bracelet to swine?"

Dagobert Hastings stopped chewing, his sunken-cheeked face registering nothing. "To quote you, Mr. Fargo, I don't get it."

"Just a bad joke," Fargo said, dismissing the topic.

After breakfast Stan went outside to hitch the teams to Pullman's freight wagon and Sebastian's mail coach. Fargo went out back of the house to the lean-to shared by Cranky Man and Cecil.

He found the Choctaw demolishing a plate of eggs and fried potatoes.

"What'd you do with the kid?" Fargo said. "Shoot him?"

"He's in the corral combing the witches' bridles out of our horses' manes. That little freckle-faced fucker is starting to chap my ass. I shoulda let him burn up."

"Look," Fargo said, "I want you to—"

"Go to hell, Fargo! I walked guard last night from ten to midnight and then lost more sleep in that Fayetteville deal. Then that little bitch Malinda kept me awake barking like a dog while you poured the wood to her. I'm crawling right back in them blankets when I finish this feed."

"Simmer down, you grumpy son of a bitch. I was going to say, I want you to grab some shut-eye. When you wake up I want you to get the Greener and a few shells from Marcella."

Cranky Man belched and farted at the same time. Fargo backed up and kicked the door open, fanning the air in front of his face.

"Take the gun," he continued, "and lie low in one of the stock sheds. Watch for anybody riding in. You got sharp eyes— if you see badges, haul your freight into my room and hide under the bed."

Cranky Man wiped his mouth on the back of his hand. "You expect the law?"

"Depends how things work out with that drunk guard. If you spot Scofields riding in, fill 'em full of blue whistlers. You won't need to be a good aim with that scattergun."

"And it don't matter one jackstraw if *I* get killed, right?"

Fargo grinned wickedly. "Not really. You're just an Indian."

By the time Fargo went outside in the yard Pullman had already left for his freight run to the Mountainberg relay station. Lonny Munro made a final examination of the Concord's hub nuts and spokes and made sure all the iron tires were snug to the wood.

"She's ready to roll!" he called up to Sebastian, who was tugging on his buckskin gauntlets.

His Henry in his right hand, Fargo grabbed the rung and hoisted himself onto the box to the left of Sebastian. Sebastian snapped the lines and the swift wagon lurched into motion.

"Fargo," he said, "I'm a sunny son of a buck by nature. But I got a bad feeling about this run. A *mighty* bad feeling."

14

Ozark West Transfer made a daily run between the mail-sorting station in Fayetteville and the Butterfield relay station at West Fork in the rugged Devil's Den region of Northwest Arkansas. The distance was not great, but the terrain was often steep with sharp, dangerous turns and sheer drop-offs requiring drivers with consummate skills.

All but one of the three seats had been removed from the sturdy Concord coach whipped by Sebastian Kilroy, making room for the dozens of mail sacks and small parcels now piled into it. Six strong mules were harnessed for the run, and they were making good time as the coach headed due south along Old Granville Pike.

"There's a big stirring and to-do over this newfangled Pony Express due to start up in a few weeks," Sebastian called over to Fargo. "But it ain't nothing but a showboat. *Five dollars* to carry a one-ounce letter! Mister, that's damn near a week's wages for most workers."

"It's a stunt," Fargo agreed. "Alexander Majors hired me last year to help sight the route through. He admitted it's just to build excitement about his freight-hauling firm and he expects to take a big loss on it."

"Them skinny boys with leather mail pouches can't handle no volume, neither. Heck, mail going to and from the Comstock alone fills dang near a coach a day."

Fargo's sun-slitted eyes stayed in constant motion. This first part of the route, with steep, brush-covered slopes on both sides of the wagon road, made for a dry-gulcher's paradise.

But Fargo expected any trouble to be a few miles farther

ahead where the Ozark region suddenly transformed itself dramatically. And as they topped the next rise, much of that region suddenly lay spread out before them like a giant diorama.

"There she is," Sebastian remarked. "Devil's Den. I call it Satan's garden."

The savagely beautiful terrain lay under a morning sun turned a smoky red by thick cloud cover: mountains sliced by ravines, stunning rock formations, high bluffs and cascading waterfalls. A deep valley lay at the heart of it with a silver ribbon of creek frothing and winding through it.

It never failed, Fargo thought. It seemed like every stunning part of the West fell prey to outlaws, business "consortiums" or both. Out west in the High Sierra, hydraulic miners with their "dictators," giant, high-pressure hoses, were literally washing away the beauty; entire regions were being denuded of timber, turning them into erosion wastelands; peaceful settlers were being run off their farms by hired thugs claiming huge tracts of land stolen for the railroad barons by acts of Congress.

The road dipped again and the rugged vista disappeared.

"These two old maids," said Sebastian, whose greatest addiction was corny jokes, "was reminiscing about their courtin' and sparkin' days. 'As a girl,' says one, 'I had four sweethearts.'

" 'All tolled?' says the other.

" 'No,' says the first old gal, 'one managed to keep his mouth shut.'"

Fargo, still scrutinizing both sides of the narrow road, chuckled politely. But his mind was on something else. Because Sebastian had been knocked out night before last, Fargo believed he could not have been involved in the barn burning—if in fact any Ozark West employee had been, an assumption Fargo was not willing to make. He now decided to trust the veteran driver.

"Tell me straight from the shoulder, Sebastian," he said. "Are you suspicious of any of the workers at Ozark West?"

The driver glanced over at him, wary. "How do you mean?"

"Look, you know why Marcella hired me. And I think you know that expensive bracelet was stolen from a secret drawer in her desk that outsiders wouldn't likely know about. It must have at least occurred to you that it might've been an inside job."

He nodded reluctantly. "Yeah, but I got no one man in mind for it. And I knew that wasn't no 'bad joke' when you asked the Professor about it at breakfast this morning."

"No, I was just fishing. But what about Dagobert? You've been around him for years—you must have an opinion."

"I ain't never much liked him, personally speaking. But he was a strong right arm to old Tubby, and he's got the inside track with Marcella. She couldn't run the show without him—not yet, anyhow."

"Does he keep honest books?"

"Far as I know. Tubby was no hand at ciphering, but he was way too smart to be short-changed, and Marcella's got a mind like a steel trap. Tell you the straight, though, it knocked me galley west when the will was read out."

"Why's that?"

"We all figured the Professor would inherit at least a piece of the business. He was there from the get-go and helped Tubby build it up from scratch."

"Interesting," Fargo said.

"Don't get me wrong, Skye. The Professor drives me to pure distraction, alla time talking like a book and using them store-bought words. But I got no reason to believe there's larceny in his soul."

"Same here," Fargo admitted. "But something ain't quite jake and I can't get a loop around it. It's not just the bracelet. There's also the barn fire—I'm told that Lem Scofield is an arsonist, and if that's so I like him for the crime."

"I'd lay odds on him, too."

"But that was a dark, cloudy night, and the Scofields wouldn't likely have known so soon that we set up an all-night guard. Yet you were knocked into a cocked hat. It's just a hunch, but it picks at me like a burr."

Sebastian nodded thoughtfully. "That is a mite queer, ain't it? And it just so happens I was conked when I was nowhere near the barn."

"About that bracelet," Fargo said. "I've got an idea where it might be. A couple days back me and Cranky Man did a good scout of the layout around Devil's Den. I found fresh tracks at the entrance of Devil's Den Cave."

"Them Scofield boys know them caves real good," Sebastian chimed in.

"So I hear. Anyhow, when I started to go inside, somebody opened fire on me with a rifle. And it sounded a lot like a Big Fifty."

"Eb Scofield," Sebastian said, not making it a question.

"Yeah, that gets my money."

"Eb is a sick-brained son of a pup. But why hide that bracelet in a cave?" Sebastian wondered. "It's small enough to hide—"

He paused, forehead wrinkling. "Say, there was something else took from that drawer that's got Marcella all ex-fluctuated."

Fargo nodded. "But she won't tell anybody what it is."

"Naw, but she's worried as all get-out about it. More worried than she is 'bout going to jail over that bracelet."

The trail was climbing steeply again.

"Gee-*ah*!" Sebastian rallied the mules, snatching the whip from its socket and snapping it over the leaders' heads. "Gee-*ah*, you ugly animules!"

Fargo didn't like the look of this stretch at all. The sides had steepened above them, dwarfing the Concord. Huge boulders clustered in pockets high above, dangerous in themselves but also providing excellent snipers' nests.

The tug chains rattled, the coach swayed on its braces and the mules squealed in protest at the steep grade and cracking whip. Fargo suddenly felt the back of his neck tighten and tingle—that sixth sense for danger that the old mountain men called a "truth goose."

Fargo craned his neck to watch the rock-strewn slope above them.

One man, a second, flashed into view.

Fargo tossed the butt of the Henry into his shoulder socket, working the lever and expecting gunfire from above. Instead, a boulder the size of a small stove abruptly leaped into motion, crashing and bouncing as it hurtled toward the wagon road. The slope seemed to heave and shake like a giant waking up as the juggernauting boulder pulled a wall of rocks with it.

"Rockslide!" Fargo shouted, his blood turning to ice water. "Light a fire under those jennies, Sebastian!"

Fargo realized their situation could not be more hazardous. They were already pulling up a steep grade, and the precipitate sides had them hemmed in tight. It was too late to rein to a stop, and the only option was to try to outrun the slide.

And given its quickly gathering speed and force, Fargo considered that more of a miracle than an option.

Sebastian glanced up and turned so white, he looked as if he'd been drained by leeches. He braced his feet against the dashboard and made his buckskin whip fairly hum.

"Gee-*ah*!" he bellowed above the growing din of the rockslide. "Gee-*ah*! *Whoop*! Gerlong there, *whoop*!"

A good reinsman always cracked his snake over the mules' heads, never striking them. But now a desperate Sebastian lashed their rumps. The enraged mules squealed in protest but surged slightly faster against gravity.

But Fargo knew it wasn't enough—stagecoach, men and mules were about to be crushed to a greasy paste. There was only one chance, and it was so slim that the Trailsman considered it a will-o'-the-wisp.

Slim, however, was still better than nothing where certain death was the price of surrender. Fargo wasted no precious seconds debating the matter.

He dropped his rifle, stood up on the box, gathered himself and leaped onto the backs of the wheel team.

It was like trying to stand up on rolling logs, and for a few awful seconds Fargo fought for his balance as he teetered on the brink of falling under the wheels.

The rapidly approaching tidal wave of rocks sounded like a roaring blizzard, and Fargo recovered his balance and desperately leaped onto the next team, then the leaders. As the vanguard of the rocks began pelting the coach like giant hailstones, Fargo straddled the back of the nearside mule, bent forward and clamped his teeth hard on one of its long, tender ears.

"Run, you dumb son of a bitch!" he bellowed.

Even the increasing din of the slide, the growing racket as ever-larger rocks ricocheted hard off the coach, could not drown out the enraged mule's explosive squeal of rage.

Balancing himself precariously, Fargo stretched over and gave the same treatment to the offside leader.

A rock slammed into Fargo's upper arm, instantly numbing it; another whizzed past his head so close, it skewed his hat. Behind him Sebastian cursed, the coach rocked crazily and the mules squealed all around him as if they were under the blade.

It's too damn late, Fargo despaired, waiting for the crushing death that now loomed over them.

But his desperate trick had worked. The agitated mules had surged just enough to pull them clear as the main gather of the slide exploded onto the trail behind them in a choking wall of yellow-brown dust.

Fargo hung on to the mule until Sebastian reached the top of the grade and the trail leveled off. He kicked on the brake and reined in.

Massaging his sore arm, Fargo hopped down. Sebastian, pouring sweat, mopped his face with his bandanna. He swung down off the box.

"Moses on the mountain, Skye! You pulled us through! I never seen the like in all my born days!"

"The mules did the pulling, old son. I just motivated 'em a little."

"I see you got winged," Sebastian said, watching Fargo rub his arm. "Is it serious?"

"Long way from my heart," Fargo said dismissively. "You all right?"

"Well, I might have to change my drawers. But I never got touched, thanks to you. I see a couple of the mules got dinged up, though, and the coach has a few battle scars. But Jesus!"

Sebastian looked behind and below them, where rocks and small boulders now formed a choke point in the narrow road.

"You think it was man-caused, Skye?"

"No 'think' about it. It was s'pose to pass for a natural slide. But I saw two men up there right before it started."

"Scofields." Sebastian spat the word out as if it had a bad taste. "Put up to it by Anslowe Deacon."

"The way you say," Fargo agreed.

"And, see, it works out perfect for Deacon. He uses the

main freight road just like Ozark West does. But only we use this cutoff to West Fork. Well, the mail will get through today. But Ozark West is over a barrel. Pete sakes, we can't even get back to the station, let alone deliver any more mail, until that road is cleared."

Fargo nodded. "Deacon wants that Butterfield mail contract like they want ice water in hell. He'll figure Ozark West is finished now."

"Ain't we?" Sebastian said bitterly. "We'll need a powder man to blow that trail clear."

"He won't be able to blow it clear," Fargo said. "Take a closer look down there, Sebastian. That trail is like the narrow end of a funnel."

"Yeah . . . yeah, I take your drift. There ain't no place to blow them rocks to. It'll all have to be hauled out. That would be a mort of work and take a mort of time. And no mail can run till it's cleared."

"You throw down your hand too quick," Fargo chided him. "West Fork is less than a mile from here, right?"

"Not even a half mile."

"All right. First we finish delivering the mail, and we leave word for Butterfield there's been a rockslide. Whether it was deliberate or not ain't nothing to the matter, right? Either way it's not Ozark West's fault."

"I reckon that's so. Rockslides are common on freight and mail routes."

"For a fact. So we tell them there's going to be a brief delay with the mail, but *very* brief."

Sebastian rubbed his chin. "How can we back that claim?"

"You mentioned a powder man—do you know of one?"

"Sure. Carl Baumgarter in Fayetteville. We've used him a few times before and he's a top hand. But—"

"But me no buts. Look at that slide again. Momentum took most of the rocks to the east side of the trail. A powder man will know how to shape his charge. He won't have to blow the rocks out of the trail—he just blows out the base of the slope on the *west* side of the trail. You only need about a hundred feet of detour to get around that mess."

Sebastian's face brightened. "Sure! It would take a small

crew of laborers with shovels and wheelbarrows less than a day to grade a crude bypass wide enough for a coach."

"Now you're whistling. Think we can borrow a couple of saddle mules at West Fork?"

"I know we can. Slappy Grabowitz runs the Butterfield relay there, and him and me go way back in these parts."

Fargo nodded. "Mules are sure-footed and can get us over those rocks. We'll leave the coach at West Fork and ride back to the station."

"I ain't so sure," Sebastian hedged, "that Marcella can pay for a powder man and a work crew right now."

"She'll bill Butterfield for the powder man," Fargo said. "They can afford it, and it's their mail. And you, me and Cranky Man are her work crew. We'll use the buckboard to get the tools up here. Now let's cut the chin-wag and get this swift wagon rolling."

"Cranky Man?" Sebastian repeated dubiously as he snapped the lines. "You told me that Injin hates hard work."

"Not when he's paid in joy juice."

"One thing still pricks at me, Skye. What if the Scofield boys just blow the trail shut somewheres else?"

Fargo set his lips in a grim, determined slit. "It's my job to discourage that idea. And I'm gonna get right on it."

15

Fargo moved into action quickly the next morning.

"Haul your lazy red ass out of bed," he called out, kicking Cranky Man's foot.

The bleary-eyed Choctaw started half awake, mind still clogged with the cobwebs of slumber, and reached for the knife sheathed behind his neck. Fargo, anticipating this reaction, caught his arm by the wrist.

"Snap into it," Fargo ordered. "We got a long day ahead of us."

Cranky Man, inventing new curses, sat up on his pallet. He glanced past Fargo to the open door of the lean-to.

"Fargo, you sorry sack of shit! The sun ain't even up!"

"You told me once that you get up with the birds and lie down with the pigs," Fargo quipped cheerfully.

"Mr. Fargo," said a sleepy young voice behind Fargo, "why would Cranky Man lie down with pigs?"

In his hurry Fargo had forgotten about Cecil.

"It's just a manner of speaking," Fargo replied awkwardly. "Sorry I woke you up."

"That's all right. Are you gonna be doing some shootin' today?"

"Not if I can help it."

"He's a liar," Cranky Man grumped as he pulled on his moccasins. "Before this day is over somebody will have a sucking chest wound. All right, Fargo, what's the play?"

"You might say we're gonna take a spoke from Anslowe Deacon's wheel."

Cecil thumbed a rough crumb of sleep from one eye, looking even more confused. "Taking one spoke from a wheel won't—"

"Again, kid, it's just a manner of speaking," Fargo impatiently cut the boy off. "It means to pay him back in kind, give him a dose of his own medicine, that type of deal."

Cranky Man pushed to his feet and stuffed his New Haven Arms converted revolver into his waistband. "What's for breakfast?"

"It ain't ready yet. We're riding out now—you can gnaw on some cold biscuits."

Fargo pushed the protesting Choctaw outside into the grainy half-light.

"You're a contrary son of a bitch," Fargo said as they headed toward the corral to saddle up. "You're not drawing wages to laze around eating and sleeping."

Fargo ducked behind a stock shed and began stripping off his buckskins.

"Strip down," he ordered the Choctaw.

Cranky Man narrowed his eyes in suspicion. "Strip? Just what *am* I drawing wages for?"

Fargo tossed him a pair of trousers and a shirt. "I borrowed these last night from Stan and Sebastian. Put 'em on and wear this floppy hat so it covers your face good. We're going to waylay one of Deacon's freight wagons, but I want you to hold back from the road so the driver can't see you're an Indian."

"I'll wear the pants and hat. But my sheath is sewed into my shirt, and I ain't giving up my knife."

"Yeah, that's right. All right, everything but the shirt."

"You crazy bastard," Cranky Man said as he followed orders. "You won't be happy till you see me hang."

"It ain't the worst way to die so long as they place the knot right."

The two men rode out as the sun broke over the eastern rim. They rode five miles south on Old Granville Pike until Fargo reined in at a thick covert of pine and dogwood trees.

"Sebastian says the first Fort Smith Express freight wagon will roll past here shortly," Fargo explained. He pulled a corked bottle of coal oil from a saddle pocket. "But it ain't gonna reach Van Buren."

"This shit's for the birds," Cranky Man groused. "Soon as this deal is over I'm getting outside of some grub and then going back to bed."

Fargo turned his face away to hide a sly grin. The Choctaw would get a good meal, all right, and he'd need it. Fargo didn't have the heart to tell him yet that he would spend the better part of today—and likely tomorrow—busting his hump on the West Fork cutoff in Devil's Den.

Sebastian was riding into Fayetteville early to line up that powder man, and Fargo intended to finish the bypass around the rockslide as quickly as possible.

"I hear the wagon," Fargo announced less than a half hour later. He pulled his bandanna over his face. "You stay back here with the horses. But watch everything out on the road close—Deacon might have an ace or two up his sleeve."

Fargo jacked a round into the Henry's chamber. When the wagon was almost abreast of the covert he stepped out into the road.

"Rein it in," he shouted to the driver, "or I'll turn you into a sieve!"

The driver hauled back on the lines and kicked the brake. "Don't shoot, mister! I got a family to feed!"

"That's mighty touching. Real easy, toss down that hog-leg," Fargo ordered, meaning the big Colt percussion side-arm the driver wore in a canvas holster.

"Sure, mister, I ain't no hero."

Fargo, keeping a close eye on the driver as he pulled out the hog-leg, was a fractional second too late to react in time when a man popped up over the sideboards of the wagon, a double-ten express gun leveled at the Trailsman.

An eyeblink later the guard loosed a cry shrill as a panther when Cranky Man's narrow-bladed throwing knife buried itself to the hilt in the man's left eye socket.

As Fargo had whirled toward this new danger the driver's sidearm was already out of the holster. He jerked the trigger and the cap cracked, but the powder failed to ignite.

"Don't shoot, mister!" he begged again, tossing the big Colt down as if he were holding the wrong end of a red-hot branding iron.

Cranky Man's knife had punctured the guard's brain and killed him instantly, a thick rope of blood squirting from his eye as he toppled over the sideboards and landed in an ungainly heap in the road.

Fargo wagged the barrel of the Henry at the white-faced driver. "Climb down. Try one more fox play and you'll fry everlasting."

"Don't kill me, mister, please! I didn't—"

"Caulk up."

Fargo propped his Henry against the wagon and shucked out his Colt. Then he picked up the hog-leg and examined it.

"Mister, can you even pour pee out of a boot? This powder ain't just clumped—it's caked solid. When's the last time you checked it?"

"I didn't know I had to. I ain't never fired it."

Fargo knocked the caps off the nipples and handed it back to him. "You best get into a safer line of work. Now park that wagon off the road to the right. Then unhitch those mules and slap 'em on the rumps."

"Yessir! *Please* don't shoot me!"

"Bottle all that female whining and do what I told you."

Fargo had picked this spot because it was one of the few places where the road widened and there was nothing close by that would burn. The frightened driver pulled the wagon out of the road and had the mules freed and scattered in jig time.

"You're taking a message to Anslowe Deacon," Fargo said.

"Yessir."

"Tell him he best call off the dogs. If his shit jobbers interfere with one more Ozark West conveyance, he'll never get another load through. You got that?"

"Yessir. Who should I say it's from?"

"Just say it's from the Eye That Never Sleeps."

The man's jaw slacked open. "You don't mean . . . ?"

"You heard me, dick weevil. Now fan the breeze before I start thinking too much about how you tried to shoot me."

The man took off running back toward Fayetteville. Cranky Man stepped out from the trees.

"Fargo, what was that crazy shit about an eye that never sleeps?"

"It's crazy to you, but every white man knows what it means. That's the motto of Allan Pinkerton's detective agency."

Fargo knew Deacon was too smart to buy it. Pinkerton agents were kept on a tight leash and would never be allowed to burn a freight wagon. But Deacon's workers weren't that smart. All they likely knew was that once Pinkerton took on a case, he brought all the little cogs down with the big wheels.

Cranky Man put one foot on the dead man's neck and yanked his knife out with a squishy, sucking sound. He wiped the blade off on the corpse's pant leg.

"That's the second time I've saved your hide," he told Fargo, "though I'm damned if I know why."

Fargo grinned. "That's why you're a good man to take along, chief, despite the stench blowing off you. Go fetch that coal oil while I see what's in the wagon."

Fargo dropped the big tailgate and laughed out loud. The entire load was fancy duds from Brooks Brothers clothiers in New York. Not only an expensive loss but excellent fuel for a hot fire.

Five minutes later the two horsemen were loping their mounts back to the Ozark West station while a thick black column of smoke rose high into the sky behind them.

Fargo's calculations proved out: Carl Baumgarter, the powder man from Fayetteville, did an expert job blowing out the base of the embankment on the West Fork cutoff.

Fargo, Sebastian and Cranky Man spent the rest of that day, and half of the next, hauling out dirt and rocks and leveling the new bypass enough to allow the mail coach through. Thus the mail was delayed only one full day.

"Mr. Fargo," Marcella said when the tired, grimy men returned to the Ozark West station and Fargo visited her in her office, "I can't find the words to thank you. When I hired you I never anticipated you'd be doing backbreaking labor."

"Well, I was hired to keep your coaches and wagons moving," Fargo replied. "So it's all part of the job description. Ask you a favor?"

"Certainly."

"Do you figure you know me well enough to call me Skye? I get nervous when people call me mister."

Those gorgeous green eyes, usually blazing with indignation, now sparkled.

"Yes, Skye. After the way I shamelessly stared at you the night you . . . frolicked with my sister, it does seem silly to be so formal."

"Shameless? I liked it just fine when you stared."

Her pretty face, fetchingly framed by strawberry blond ringlets, flushed pink. "There was certainly plenty to take in. I didn't think I was ever going to be able to shut that door."

"I wish," Fargo assured her, "you had shut it from the inside."

An awkward silence wedged itself between them, and Fargo decided to change the subject.

"Marcella, this is the ninth day I've been working for you. That means you go to court in five days."

"Oh, don't I know it! To borrow a phrase from my mother, I'm sitting in the anxious seat. Dagobert thinks there isn't enough evidence to convict me, and he's quite intelligent, but I am not so sanguine as he."

Fargo held back from commenting on Dagobert's counsel or his possible motive for making Marcella believe all was hunky-dory.

"Farther west," Fargo said, "you wouldn't be going to court and wouldn't even have been charged with anything. A woman's word is always accepted. And since juries are all men, there's a good chance they'll vote for acquittal here in Arkansas. This may be a state, but this part of it is still the wild-and-woolly frontier."

"I pray you're right. Obviously that bracelet will never turn up. But even if I'm acquitted, my name has already been tainted and a cloud of suspicion will always hang over me. And then there's— Well, never mind."

"You're worried about that bracelet, all right," Fargo said. "But you're even more worried about whatever else was stolen with it. You're scared to death, aren't you, that it will come to light?"

She nodded, rose from the chair behind her desk, and began nervously pacing, unable to meet his eyes.

"Evidence of a crime?" Fargo coaxed.

"No. Far worse. Please don't ask me what it is. But if it falls into Anslowe Deacon's hands, I . . . I wouldn't be able to face the consequences of public disclosure. More than Ozark West will be ruined. Mr. Far— I mean, Skye, I will take my own life if that happens."

"You don't really mean that?"

"I mean it as surely as we're both in this room."

Fargo studied the abject fear and misery in her face and concluded that she meant every word.

"Marcella, I don't know who got into that secret drawer or if he had help from one of your workers. Right now that doesn't matter. But I have a hunch, *just* a hunch, that Eb Scofield was the thief. And I think I *might* know where he hid both items. Not exactly where, but generally."

She whirled toward him. "Where?"

"Never mind that. You're charged with stealing the bracelet, so it doesn't help your cause to know where it might be."

"Yes, I take your point."

"As to that other item you're being so mysterious about— I'd say Scofield hasn't told Deacon about it."

"But why do you believe that?"

"Lady, you just got done saying that if Deacon had it he could ruin you *and* Ozark West. Do you really believe, given all the grief I've already rationed out to him and that Scofield trash, he wouldn't have played that card now if it was in his hand?"

"Why . . . why, no, of course not! Why burn down our barn and cause rockslides and take the risk of killing Jimbo Miller and all the rest of it if he could succeed quickly and effortlessly? Skye, I think you're absolutely right!"

"I hope so but put away the hats and horns. Remember, if Eb does have it, he could put the crusher on you anytime by giving or selling it to Deacon."

"Oh, Skye, will you try to get it before that happens?"

"I'm riding out as soon as I wash up. I hope Cranky Man isn't too drunk to ride with me—I might need a second pair of eyes."

"Perhaps," she said, "it wasn't wise to bribe him with two bottles of whiskey for his hard labor."

Fargo grinned. "Sure it was. Knowing there'd be knock-um stiff waiting when we finished the job, he worked like a demon. But listen, Marcella: don't you think you ought to tell me what I'm looking for?"

Scarlet pinpoints leaped into her cheeks and she averted her gaze.

"Believe me, Skye, you'll know when you find it."

16

The northwestern Ozarks surrounded them like solid sentries as Fargo and Cranky Man descended into the sandstone crevice and cave area at the heart of the Devil's Den region.

"Why do I feel like there's a bull's-eye painted on my back?" Cranky Man remarked.

"Because there is," Fargo replied. "That's why I brought you. Takes at least one gun off of me."

"That ain't a joke, is it?"

"Sebastian tells the jokes, not me."

Cranky Man touched his magic pebbles. "Fargo, you son of a bitch. Zif that ain't bad enough, you ain't even been giving me my half of the pay."

"Why bother? I don't want to rob your corpse, so I just hold on to it. Besides, you're an ignorant savage who can't manage his wampum."

"You son of a bitch," Cranky Man repeated.

Layers of sandstone, shale and limestone were exposed to view all around them. The severe erosion had also buckled the ground into deep crevices. They trotted their mounts down farther into the valley and across a log-and-stone bridge spanning the flood-prone creek.

Cranky Man said, "You think Marcella Scott is giving you the straight arrow 'bout that bracelet?"

Fargo nodded, keeping his eyes to all sides. "She's holding back on whatever else was stolen, but she didn't take the bracelet."

"You would speak up for her. I heard you two going at it last night."

"In the first place," Fargo countered, "I don't need to speak up for a woman just to enjoy her favors. Hell, I've screwed murderers. In the second place, that wasn't Marcella."

"Then it was Malinda again. The hell was that loud crash I heard and then all that giggling?"

Fargo's lips twitched into a grin at the memory. "Seems we broke a bed board or two."

From here Fargo could see a few cabins made of stone and logs dotting the upper part of the valley, where floodwaters couldn't reach them. Closer at hand lay the massive blocks of sandstone that had collapsed from a hillside.

"Fargo," Cranky Man said, "*look* at all them damn caves. Even if you're right about the Scofield boys hiding stolen stuff around here, how do you know they picked Devil's Den Cave?"

"Did I ever say I knew it? You pay your money, you take your chances. That's the cave I was headed for when somebody opened fire on me. It's the longest cave, and a man can move around in it. And I found recent tracks around it."

"Needle in a haystack," Cranky Man insisted. "That night I slept in Big Ear Cave, I built a fire. Them sandstone walls are pockmarked with holes and big cracks. You could spend a year in one of them caves looking for every hidey-hole that could hold a damn bracelet. *If* it's even in there."

"I know all that. Humor me—I'm eccentric."

Fargo pointed ahead. "See that nest of limestone fragments? You're gonna wait behind that with the horses. I'm leaving the Henry with you. That's sixteen rounds and six more in your short iron. I know you can't shoot worth a plugged peso, but you can make enough noise to scare off a regiment."

They reached the shelter of the rock nest and both men swung down, hobbling their mounts. The entrance to Devil's Den Cave was about thirty yards ahead.

Earlier Fargo had made two torches by tying rags to the ends of sticks carved from green wood. Now he soaked the rags in coal oil.

"You know, Cranky Man," he said in a philosophic tone, "I hate the sound of a Big Fifty."

He broke into a headlong run over the exposed ground.

Either nobody was watching from the surrounding hills or the shot was too difficult. Fargo gained the entrance of the cave and ducked inside without hearing the decisive crack of a Sharps.

At first the bright afternoon sun penetrated far enough inside that Fargo didn't need to light a torch. These fracture caves were far less symmetrical than the hollow passages Fargo was more used to. The walls, floor and ceiling were rough and uneven, with frequent abutments and uplifts.

For at least two full minutes Fargo stood still and just listened as his eyes adjusted to the dimness. He didn't assume he was alone in the cave, especially since by now Deacon was focusing all his efforts, and hired killers, on the Trailsman.

Fargo moved farther inside, still listening and watching with the complete, absorbed attention that became second nature to frontier survivors. But before long he was forced to either give up or scratch a lucifer to life and ignite one of his torches.

He gambled on the torch. Its flame reflected eerily off the jagged, uneven walls. Fargo had no religion, but he imagined that if the devil really did have a den it might well look something like this rugged, inhospitable place.

For decades these caves had sheltered outlaws, outcasts and marauders, and occasionally Fargo spotted animal bones, bottles, even a discarded boot. But Cranky Man had been dead-on: the sandstone was so riddled with openings of every size and shape that it was impossible to search all of them.

Nonetheless, Fargo did his best as he progressed farther and farther back. Marcella Scott was up against it: five more days and she had to answer to the law for a valuable piece of jewelry Fargo didn't believe she took.

But by now he, too, was more worried about the mystery item she was too frightened or ashamed to even name. When a vibrant young woman with plenty of starch in her corset had decided that death was preferable to public exposure of that item, Fargo figured it was root hog or die. It was his job to locate it before it was turned against her.

Something caught his eye in the flickering light reflected ahead.

Fargo carefully picked his way closer. An uplift in the cave floor had formed a small . . . altar, Fargo decided for lack of a better word. Something lay atop it.

A moment later he recognized it: the object that had caught his eye was a pig-sticker, a long, sharply pointed rod with a crude hilt, used for slaughtering hogs by puncturing their hearts. And when Fargo moved even closer he saw a sheet of foolscap paper lying under it.

He pulled it out and recognized that it was a drawing done in smeared ink—and what he saw revealed in the lurid, red-orange torchlight made him forget to take his next breath.

Whoever had drawn it was obviously sick in the head but not without some talent. It depicted a naked woman with a horned devil crouching between her spread-eagled legs, part of his body still inside her private parts. And a long object resembling the pig-sticker was poised over her heart.

"What the *hell*?" Fargo said out loud, his words echoing farther back into the long cave in a mocking refrain.

Devil's Den Cave, he reminded himself. And here was the devil himself evidently emerging—or entering—a woman's sexual parts. And a pig-sticker—a slaughtering instrument—ready to kill her.

Or perhaps "sacrifice" her on this very "altar"?

Fargo studied the woman's face. Whoever had drawn it was no Rembrandt, and it could hardly be called an exact likeness. But the high Roman nose, the Persian-shaped eyes—it bore at least a passing resemblance to Marcella Scott.

Fargo recalled Sebastian's recent remark during the mail run two days ago: *Eb Scofield . . . he's a sick-brained son of a buck.*

The torch began flickering out and Fargo fired up the second one. The floor of the cave in this area was scattered with the ashes of what Fargo guessed was tobacco, widely smoked in clay pipes throughout the Ozarks. Somebody was spending plenty of time in this spot, but doing what?

Fargo folded the drawing and stuck it in his pocket. He picked up the pig-sticker and found a fissure in the wall big enough to dispose of it. He spent the next twenty minutes or so searching every possible hiding place around this spot, turning up nothing.

Fargo made his way back to the entrance and bolted toward the rock nest where Cranky Man waited with the horses.

"See anybody?" he asked the Choctaw as he removed the Ovaro's hobbles.

"Nope. I heard somebody chopping wood far off and a dog barking, is all. How 'bout you—find anything in there?"

"Man, did I." Fargo forked leather. "I'll tell you about it while we ride out. But you were right about that cave being too big to search. We're just stuffing the hog through its asshole. It's Eb Scofield who knows the answers, so pretty quick now we're going to the source."

"Word come down today from the squaw man," Stanton Scofield said around a mouthful of hog and hominy. "He's pissin' down his leg on account Fargo and the red Arab torched one of his wagons."

"That pus-gut clothes pole," Eb added. "You boys was all right here three days ago when the perfumed dandy told us to 'interrupt the timely flow of mail' or some shit. Well, Bubba and Lem done a good job of it with that rockslide on the West Fork cutoff. And now the little gal-boy says hold off on stopping the Ozark West rigs."

"We done a bang-up job," Lem bragged. "You boys shoulda seen it—Bubba rocked that big boulder outta the ground easier'n wiggling a loose tooth."

"Bang-up job, my ass," Stanton differed, pushing his empty plate aside and picking his teeth with a burnt match. "It didn't do a lick of good. That lanky son of a bitch Fargo got the mail coach rolling agin today."

It was well after dark and Stanton, Eb, Lem and Bubba had met at the cabin in Blue Holler. The mood was somber. All of Anslowe Deacon's recent talk of generous bonuses seemed like so much air pudding now.

"It ain't just the burnt-up wagon that's put ice in Deacon's silk boots," Stanton added. "He knows damn good and well that guard of his didn't tie one on and burn down his hay barn. But the law dogs arrested the guard, and ol' Fargo breaks it off inside Deacon agin."

"Well, Deacon says we can't kill no more of the Ozark West people," Eb reasoned, "and we ain't 'lowed to put the kibosh on their conveyances. So 'less we want to go back to robbing traps and such, we best kill Fargo before that milk-livered Deacon shows the white feather and gives all of it up as a bad job."

"Eb," Lem pointed out, "it don't matter what Deacon does now, y'unnerstan'? I hope we can collect wages for it, sure, but we got no choice but to kill Fargo. He—"

"Jimmy like tickle, hanh? Daddy's little man like that? Coochie-coochie-*coo*!"

Three pair of eyes slanted toward one side of the table. Bubba—grits dripping down his chin and the front of his filthy bib overalls, his idiotic, moon face glowing with plea-sure—held his big black sewer rat cuddled against his massive chest as he stimulated the rat between its rear legs. The nasty, pink-eyed rodent squirmed as if in apparent pleasure.

"Bubba," Lem said in a careful tone, "Jimmy's tail is hanging in your food. Put him back in your pocket, huh?"

"Sure, Lem. Time for Jimmy's nap. Jimmy, you bad boy! You pooped in Daddy's supper!"

Stanton turned his face away in disgust. "Katy Christ, Lem," he whispered, "'at fuckin' Bubba has cracked his gourd good this time."

Lem nodded. "Crazy as a shite-poke, cousin. I might hafta shoot him. I tried to grab that damn rat last night while Bubba was asleep. The damn thing commenced to squealing and Bubba woke up fightin' mad. We'll maybe wait and see if he rolls over on it and crushes it. Now he's talkin' 'bout finding it a damn sister."

Stanton shifted his attention from Cousin Bubba to his brother Eb. Stanton's shrewd face scrunched up in specu-lation.

"Eb," he said, "like Lem was just saying, we got to send Fargo under. But was you hiding down near them caves this afternoon like I told you, looking to see could you notch a bead on him?"

"A'course I was. He didn't show up, is all."

"Uh-hunh. You know, I seen Deputy Harney Roscoe in the Hog's Breath today."

"So what?" Eb retorted. "He's always in the saloon."

"Yeah. And he's still boilin' mad over how Fargo whupped him in that fight they had. Well, tomorrow I'm gonna learn right where Fargo sleeps—and I'm gonna tell Harney. He needs money real bad."

"They got that all-night guard," Eb pointed out.

"We got around it once before," Stanton reminded him.

"Yeah, I reckon that's so." Eb didn't like his brother's tone and dark expression.

"But here's the deal, Eb. Fargo ain't all me and Harney talked about."

"Bully for you."

"This afternoon, when you claim you was down in the Den, he seen your horse tethered back in the woods just outside of Busted Flush."

Eb's little lizard eyes refused to blink. "Harney's fulla shit."

When he was angry Stanton Scofield had a nervous tic that kept his left eye winking half shut. It twitched so rapidly now, it seemed to be sending Morse code.

"Eb, you shit-eating liar! You was layin' in wait for Marcella Scott, wasn't you? Yeah, you're all het up to poke that nifty little piece, ain'tcher?"

Eb scowled fiercely. "The *devil* is in that high-toned harlot! I'm gonna—"

He clammed up, working both hands into fists.

"You're gonna *what*?"

Eb stubbornly shook his head.

"Goddammit," Stanton snapped. "Ain't it bad nuff that Bubba has gone crazy as a loon? You got sick ideas about women, boy. Seven holes in their bodies . . . devils in their quim! Snap out of it, brother, or Fargo will end up using our guts for garters. If your big idea is to rape and kill her, shit-can it! You kill or rape a high-toned white woman in Arkansas, and we'll *all* be jerked to Jesus—Deacon, too. Flush her from your thoughts, boy."

"It's *Fargo* we got to sweat, Cousin Eb," Lem joined in. "Not the woman. Fargo's thinking up ways to kill us right now, and he's got Deacon scared spitless."

"We got no choice now, Eb," Stanton added urgently. "We

already tried to kill him, and that's our big mistake—we *tried* and didn't finish it. A man like Fargo, you get his bristles up and he'll hang in there like a hair in a biscuit. He won't never let us off the hook now. Either we kill him first or he's gonna pop all four of us plumb center just like he done Romer."

17

"If anyone requires something from one of the stores," Dagobert Hastings announced to the rest of the men at breakfast, "please add it to my list. I'll be taking the buckboard into town this morning."

"By yourself?" Fargo asked just before he forked a load of molasses-soaked pancake into his mouth.

"I go at least once a month for the supply run. Often Marcella and Malinda ride in with me. But with everything at sixes and sevens around here, I suggested they not go. Wouldn't you agree, Mr. Fargo?"

Fargo, busy chewing a huge mouthful, only nodded. But he watched the Professor closely this morning and made no effort to be subtle about it. Fargo knew that time was pressing now and that rearguard actions meant defeat for his side.

Fargo swallowed and said, "I've noticed that you take the buckboard out way more than once a month."

"I take it you've also noticed we raise no cows or chickens," Dagobert replied. "Milk, eggs, cream and cheese—these must be procured frequently, not monthly. Otherwise how would any of us enjoy the hearty repasts served here daily."

"I 'magine so," Fargo agreed.

If Fargo needed a reminder just how quickly the clock was ticking, one was tucked into his pocket right now: the sick, ominous drawing he'd found yesterday in Devil's Den Cave. Disgusting though it was, Fargo knew that Marcella had to see it. He had a scratched-out plan in mind, but he wanted her to see firsthand *why* she must assist him.

Things got too quiet for Sebastian, who couldn't stand silence at meals.

"I got a letter from the undertaker in Busted Flush," he said. "It was signed 'Eventually yours.'"

"You told that one just a few days ago," Stan complained. "First time I ever heard you repeat one."

Fargo was barely listening. Dagobert, who usually exuded the attitude of a bemused bystander around the others, was clearly working himself up for the stump. Fargo watched him take a final deep breath.

"Gentlemen, have you ever stopped to think," he said, "that *every* man is a lawbreaker?"

"I'd say that's likely," Fargo humored him on. "There's so damn many laws you can't avoid it."

"No, Mr. Fargo, even if there was only *one* law most of us would still break it. Judges, sheriffs, politicians and even clergymen—by their very nature *all* men are corrupt and criminal. It can be restrained and denied, but it is always an animating force in human behavior. It is no great secret that some of our most beautiful and exciting women are drawn to men who scorn laws."

"Maybe all men do break the law now and again," Stan reminded him, ."but there's a helluva difference between a moonshiner and a murderer."

Dagobert nodded solemnly. "Yes, a matter of degree. But criminal guilt, too, often accretes by degrees. For example, a man may involve himself in a shady enterprise only hoping to vent his spleen over a personal slight. Yet he becomes a prisoner of his own actions and, willy-nilly, by degrees he becomes a dastardly blackguard."

"Who's Willy Nilly?" Cecil asked. Stan gave him Cranky Man's plate and shooed the kid outside.

Fargo put his fork down on his plate, watching Dagobert closely. "Are you trying *not* to tell us something? That sounded like a sort of jackleg confession, to me."

Dagobert made a dismissive motion with his hand. "Nonsense! Everyone is growing too suspicious of everyone else around here. I'm merely speaking in the abstract. I'm wont to do that."

"Never mind the mealymouthing," Fargo said, his voice taking on a hard edge. "If you got something on your mind, spell it out plain."

"I have no idea what you're talking about."

"Here, I'll go first to show you what I mean by plain speaking: You thought the entire Ozark West shebang would be yours after Orrin Scott died, didn't you?"

Dagobert didn't bat an eye. "I never expected all of it, Mr. Fargo. But, yes, I did expect part ownership. I felt, and still do, that I had earned it."

"Maybe you did earn it," Fargo said indifferently. This would go nowhere, and right now the matter of Dagobert could wait. Fargo's mind kept returning to the mortal danger facing Marcella Scott and perhaps even Malinda. He knew he couldn't delay a visit to her office any longer.

Fargo poured the last of his coffee into the saucer, blew over it, and drank it in two slurping seconds.

Marcella surprised him by opening the office door and pulling him inside before he could even knock.

"Forgive me," she told him. "I left the door open and eavesdropped on breakfast. I heard your exchange with Dagobert. Even for him those remarks were positively baffling! 'A man becomes a prisoner of his own actions.' Why, it *was* almost a confession!"

"Yeah, but we don't know how it fits in—just yet. Right now, though, I want you to sit down and take a couple deep breaths. I have to show you something mighty ugly."

The oval face paled two shades and she sat in the desk chair, scared but resolute. "What is it, Skye?"

"I found this yesterday," he explained as he began unfolding the drawing, "in Devil's Den Cave. There was a tool for slaughtering pigs weighing it down. I can't prove it, but I think it's the work of Eb Scofield."

He flattened it on the desk in front of her. She showed no visible reaction for almost a minute. Then her shoulders suddenly slumped.

The wooden hopelessness in her voice, when she finally broke the excruciating silence, startled Fargo.

"He has it, Skye," she told him, choking back a sob. "Oh, merciful God! That sick, disgusting, leering Eb Scofield *has* it!"

"The bracelet?"

"No . . . yes . . . I mean, probably that too. But I'm talking about the other item that was taken from the desk."

"Now how could you know that?"

"*This* is how I know it. It 'inspired' this! I've noticed him for some time now, always watching me in town. He's sick. His eyes, they're . . . they're little, but luminous, and he—"

Her tone changed again, this time strained to the breaking point with a sudden upwelling of emotions as she added: "And, yes, I know what you're wondering: do I think the woman Scofield drew stands for me? Yes, I'm certain of it."

"All right," Fargo said. "So am I."

"What can we do about it?"

"I could just kill him. But with you in this big court deal, and all the questions that lizard-eyed killer could answer, I think it's a better idea to make him my guest for a spell."

"Your . . . ? And just how do you propose to do that?"

"That," Fargo said, "is an excellent question . . ."

The rest of Fargo's tenth day as the Ozark West troubleshooter passed without major incident. Neither Ozark West freight nor mail was hampered, and at least for the near future Marcella Scott's animal stock had good-quality hay and grain, unwilling compliments of Anslowe Deacon.

"It's you they're after now, Fargo," Cranky Man gloated as the two men smoked in his lean-to. "You're the thorn in their flesh now, Trailsman. Just like you wanted it. And I'm gonna piss on your grave."

"I expect no less," Fargo said solemnly.

"You mean Marcella is really playing along with this trap you got planned?"

"It ain't like I twisted her arm," Fargo said. "She jumped at the chance."

"So why tomorrow? If it's so all-fired important, why didn't you spring this deal today?"

Fargo stood to one side of the doorway, watching the open valley floor visible from the back of the station house. The heavily forested Ozarks hemmed the place, excellent shooting blinds for ambushers.

"Because today," Fargo replied, "Dagobert went to town by himself, remember?"

"That bandy-legged pipsqueak? He ain't got the stones to be in on any crimes."

"That's just your contrary nature speaking. You suspect him, too."

Cranky Man grunted. "Yeah. First time I saw him I felt in my bones he was no good."

Fargo's upcoming guard shift was midnight to two a.m., but he drank plenty of strong black coffee and didn't turn in. Instead he reinforced each yard sentry, beginning with Lonny Munro then Jeremiah Pullman and Cranky Man.

Like all the others, Fargo's two-hour stint passed with nothing more remarkable than a howling wolf or invading snake. He roused Sebastian at two and reinforced his watch as he had the others. Then Fargo woke Stan for the final watch.

"I'm turning in," Fargo told him. "Stan, I won't lie to you—there's reasonable odds the Scofields will make a play before full sunrise."

"Believe me," Stan assured him, "after that whack I got the night the barn burned down, I don't do no daydreaming."

Harney Roscoe kept pulling out his watch, wanting to get this shit over with.

He didn't like the way false dawn was already lifting some of the curtain of darkness. Harney had raised holy hell about the timing, but nobody won an argument with Stanton Scofield.

At least Harney was certain that Fargo was in bed by now. Shortly after the two-to-four watch ended, Roscoe had seen light flare up in his room. Only a minute later it flared out.

His horse was hobbled well behind him in the first of the screening timber. Roscoe made a final check of his watch: the yard sentry should be distracted now.

He had drawn his Remington the moment he started forward toward the house. Stanton Scofield had warned him about the lean-to where the half-breed slept. Roscoe gave it wide berth, circling back toward Fargo's open window at the rear corner of the house.

A white curtain seemed to lick at the night as vagrant breezes tugged it in and out of the window in a sinuous rhythm. Roscoe moved silently to the edge of the window frame and stood listening.

No snoring. But not all men snored.

Roscoe tucked at the knees and peered over the sill.

The room was dark, but the white counterpane on the bed seemed undisturbed by shape or light.

Roscoe didn't like this shit. Fargo had been walking guard for hours, why couldn't he just be in his fucking bed like any normal man? And where the hell *was* he?

He was about to reverse his dust, money be damned, when he suddenly recalled the roweling and mocking he had endured ever since Fargo knocked him through the front wall of the Hog's Breath. Even the soiled doves had taken to calling him Fargo's Squaw and Ass-in-the-Hole.

A surge of white-hot anger steeled Harney's purpose. He craned his neck over the sill to view the rest of the room.

Nothing. No pallets in the corners, no—

Harney's scrotum instantly shriveled when cold steel kissed his right temple.

"Peekaboo," Fargo said. "Looks like you got table stakes after all, Roscoe. So the bet's up to you."

Roscoe's Remington was still outside the window, muzzle nudging the wall right about where Fargo seemed to be crouching in the shadows.

"I bet *this*, cheese dick," the deputy retorted, the gunshot deafening when he fired through the wall point-blank.

He was still cocking the hammer when a second shot cracked the stillness, spraying bloody gobbets of Roscoe's brain inside and outside the house.

18

The two shots had roused the entire house.

"Merciful *God*," Malinda exclaimed, paling as she backed out of Fargo's room. "*I'm* not going to clean that up!"

Marcella, too, had quickly averted her eyes after Fargo fired up the lamp.

"Do you think he's in with the Scofields," Marcella said, "or just settling a personal grudge with you?"

Fargo, bare to the waist, sat on the edge of the bed and thumbed a reload into his sidearm.

"Could be one, the other, or both," he replied, watching Dagobert Hastings, one of the first to arrive.

"I don't get it, Skye," Stan spoke up. "Nobody made a play against me. I guess I just somehow missed him."

"There was *nothing* out of the ordinary about your guard watch?" Fargo pressed.

"Nah. You turned in—or said you was—at four. I walked the entire yard, including around the house, and saw or heard nothing unusual. Around a quarter to four or so Dagobert come out with a couple cups of coffee, and we talked for maybe—"

Stan fell silent, looking at Dagobert. "Yeah. He comes outside with two cups, and me and him stood near the smithy chewing the fat while we drank it. All this at the same time you was jumped, Skye."

"Dagobert," Marcella spoke up, "you told me you don't like coffee. You said it jangles your nerves."

"My cup held tea," the Professor said. "My dear, you know I love tea."

"I've never seen you take a cup of coffee to any of us

before," Stan said. "Why start with me? You don't even like me. And why weren't you asleep?"

"So it's true," Dagobert retorted. "No good deed left unpunished."

"Answer Stan's question," Fargo said. "Why, like a bolt out of the blue, does he rate a cup of coffee?"

"The Salem witch hunts are alive and well, I see."

"Since you're not answering questions," Fargo said, "here's one more. You went to town by yourself today. That's why I was ready in my room tonight. And maybe twelve hours after you go to town, Harney Roscoe knows exactly which room I'm sleeping in. Just a coincidence?"

"Correlation is not causation. And not one shred of the supposed evidence against me is probative."

"That's legal swamp gas," Fargo said. "You're a damn liar."

"I am not a liar, Mr. Fargo. I am, however, when the occasion requires it, quite adept at sophisticated strategies of evasiveness."

"Don't that just mean you're a damn good liar?" Sebastian demanded.

"Never mind," Fargo said. "I'm sick of his smirking face. Don't you see it? That last remark of his was another one of those wormy, jackleg confessions. When we're done here, Stan, I want you to escort the Professor to his room. Then—"

"Mr. Fargo," Dagobert protested, "this is America. Before you assume a man's guilt, you must make assurances doubly sure."

"That's what I'm doing," Fargo said. "Stan, like I was saying—escort the Professor to his room. Wrap him up tight in one of his sheets and then, to be *doubly sure*, tie him up good around the arms and ankles."

"Marcella," Dagobert protested, "this is *your* station. Has this man taken over?"

"The security, yes. And I don't like the way you're behaving, either."

"Tell you what, Dagobert," Fargo said. "Getting tied up is the least of your troubles."

"Meaning what? That you plan to hang me in the absence of evidence or a trial?"

"Oh, you might end up *begging* for a noose, bookworm. There're things so hard on a man's body that hanging by the neck would seem like going to heaven. Marcella and I have a little plan for later today. If it works, Eb Scofield falls into our hands. If it comes a cropper, then *you* will be the one."

"The one . . . what?"

"You best just pray that our plan works. Because I'm sick and damn tired of always waiting for the ricochets. *Pray* that we grab Eb. Because if we don't, I'm getting the truth out of you even if I have to slow-roast your brains over hot coals."

When the sun was well up Fargo flung his chair over his shoulder and went out into the corral to tack the Ovaro. He rolled Harney Roscoe's body into an old groundsheet and lashed it behind his cantle. He forked leather and rode into Busted Flush.

"Christ, Fargo," Sheriff Dub Gillycuddy muttered, quickly turning his face away. "You blew off half the front of his skull."

"He was blasting away at me through the wall. Pardon me all to hell and back if I couldn't shoot him in a spot more to your liking. At least now you know he had some brains."

Fargo dropped the flap of groundsheet back into place and the two men went into the sheriff's cubbyhole office.

"I expected this," the lawman said. "Harney's been talkin' chummy with Stanton Scofield. And Harney's been hot-jawing you ever since you pounded the paste outta him. He is—was—the type who always has to be nursing a grudge. He really was a worthless son of a bitch."

Gillycuddy sighed and sat on one corner of his desk. "Well, Fargo, at least you're making the undertaker happy. That's two deaths now for locals to get all riled up about. I told you to keep the killings far away from town."

"That's not too easy when the killers don't arrange their schedules with me. Look, you heard of any warrants for me in Fayetteville?"

The sheriff chuckled. "You done a good job on that score, buckskins. Deacon never did go to law over that business where you shot up the knees of his worker. He couldn't on account his Cherokee whore killed a white man in the same

119

fracas, and he couldn't chance losing her. She ain't just his night woman—she's a damn good bodyguard."

"Yeah, well, you're preaching to the converted. She damn near gutted me."

"And when you burnt his feed barn down—no, don't shake your head; I know you done it—Deacon couldn't stop the law from mixing into it. But the Fayetteville sheriff had nothing to go on. That poor clodhopper you got drunk never once saw or named you, and his story sounded made-up."

"I got no idea what you're talking about," Fargo said from a poker face.

"If it gets any deeper in here I'll have to send for the honey wagon."

"I heard Anslowe didn't prosecute that clodhopper."

"Why would he? *He* knew the story was true."

"And nothing about the freight wagon that somebody burnt up?" Fargo prompted.

"Nope. I figure Deacon's got too much dirt on his hands by now to count on the law covering for him. 'Less you count this trial coming up for Marcella Scott in just a few days."

"I count it," Fargo said. "And so does she. You heard anything on that deal?"

"Not a damn thing. But Anslowe Deacon ain't getting the good newspaper write-ups he used to. There's a couple ink-slingers asking questions 'bout Tubby Scott's death. I hear the mayor of Fayetteville ain't seen so often these days with Deacon."

The sheriff pulled a drawstring pouch and papers from his vest pocket and began building a cigarette.

"With all the hearsay peddlers keeping this deal at a boil," he resumed as he crimped a paper, "there's a chance the jury will see that bracelet as a frame-up."

Fargo agreed. But that did nothing to solve Marcella's self-torture about whatever else was missing.

"Tell me, Dub—just how rough are these Scofields?"

"Truth to tell, I never had the balls to tangle with them." Gillycuddy licked the paper. "They ain't got your smarts and guts, Skye, but they're plenty dangerous. Now Bubba, he ain't got even one oar in the water, but he'll eat his own guts if his brother, Lem, tells him to. If he ever pins your arms, you're going to glory."

Fargo said, "Lem is the fire-starter. Would you rate him a danger in a frolic?"

"Yes, dammit, because the little runt is tricky and sneaky. He's a back-shooter, and while the rest are keeping you distracted, he'll sneak up behind you."

The lawman lit his cigarette, watching Fargo. "Eb and Stanton are the most dangerous. They was both in the Mexican war and they're stone-cold killers. It's true that Stanton struts around with his Colt Navy tied low, putting on like he's a big gun-thrower. He ain't, but the man really is fast."

"Yeah, these herky-jerky nervous types often are."

"I seen him pull that widow-maker of his back in a fair fight against Red Mike Meadows, that two-gun slick out of Baton Rouge. Meadows had him a reputation building for some kills in New Orleans, but Stanton cut him down before Red Mike's gun cleared leather."

The sheriff threw back his head and blew three perfect smoke rings. "That's why I smoke," he boasted. "Look at them fuckers—perfect doughnuts."

He looked at Fargo again and his tone turned serious.

"As to Eb Scofield . . . you already know he's some pumpkins with a Big Fifty. And never mind that he's touched— that son of a bitch is sneaky just like Lem. Mister, I mean *cunning*. Keep that Choctaw pard of yours sober and covering your back, Fargo. I can tell the showdown is coming, and that bunch will likely force you down to Devil's Den for the deathblow. They know that region better than most men who live there."

"That's nice to hear," Fargo said as he headed toward the door. "I s'pose most men prefer to be buried in familiar country."

"You're cocky," the sheriff called to his back, "and you've earned it. But I mean it, Fargo: the Scofield boys are toothless trash who can't read or cipher, but don't underrate them as devious killers."

19

It was a hot, sunny afternoon, so breezeless the trees stood still as paintings. Marcella Scott was nicely turned out in a cream taffeta dress, lace shawl and scalloped bonnet.

Fargo had encouraged her to pick a dress that would emphasize her womanly surfaces and suggest a "fast young lady," to employ Dagobert's term—the devil's consort, as Eb Scofield saw her. Now, as she drove the buckboard toward Busted Flush, her strawberry blond hair sun-shimmered, a mass of coils and ringlets flowing out of the bonnet.

Two men riding mules from the direction of town barely spread out in time when the buckboard sailed between them. They stared in slack-jawed amazement behind the eye-pleasing sight of Marcella as she continued toward Busted Flush.

"I don't see any Scofields," she said aloud, apparently to herself. Her voice sounded nervous but determined.

"Scofields? If we run into the whole pack at once," replied a male voice from the bed behind her, muffled by a patchwork quilt, "we're going to regret this little stunt."

"Regret . . . ? But, Skye, surely you considered that possibility?"

"Actually," his muted voice admitted, "I didn't. I'll leave it up to you. I suspect Eb is champing at the bit for a chance to nab you and that he spends plenty of time alone watching for you. But this is risky and you're free to change your mind."

Marcella recalled the drawing Fargo had shown her, the work of an ugly, twisted, demented mind. She reminded herself, too, that she knew exactly what had set Eb Scofield's sick mind off, and heat flooded her face.

"No, I find the risk acceptable," she said. "I agree that Eb is the key. But do you really plan to torture him, Skye, if he won't cooperate? You hinted as much to Dagobert."

"I don't think it'll go that far. But, yeah, I'd torture Eb or Dagobert if I had to. Now let's cut the chin-wag—you're s'pose to be alone."

The buckboard bounced through a stretch of washboard road, throwing Fargo around like a mail sack. It was stifling under the quilt. He cursed his own plan and wished he could just move on. The Ozarks always spelled trouble for him.

"We're coming into town," Marcella said. "What now?"

"Run a simple errand or two, show yourself. He can't take the bait unless he sees it."

"Take the bait? Yes, I suppose that's what I am," she said, her tone bitter and tired.

"For now, yeah. Don't be a fool in town. Stop only where there're witnesses, and don't stroll too far from the buckboard."

The conveyance rattled to a stop, and Fargo felt it rock slightly as she lit down. Hot sun beating down on the thick quilt left Fargo clammy with sweat. The quilt smelled like manure.

About ten minutes later the buckboard again rocked slightly when Marcella climbed onto the leather-padded seat. She clucked to the team and Fargo jogged slightly when the rig jerked into motion.

"Skye," came her strained voice, "Eb spotted me when I came out of the milliner's. He's mounting his horse now."

"That's what we want," Fargo called to her. "Just stay calm and keep leading him out of town."

But Fargo knew Marcella could hardly feel calm. He had discussed this crucial moment with her—if they were right in their guess, Eb was determined to abduct her and take her to Devil's Den, not kill her outright close to Busted Flush.

If they were wrong, Eb could just shoot her before Fargo could do a damn thing about it. But Fargo wagered on the man's brain sickness—a man like Eb wouldn't just shoot a woman who copulated with devils; he would have to *cleanse* her, purify her, punish her, all the time staring at her luscious nakedness and declaring his own lust hell-spawned.

"He's gaining on us rapidly now," Marcella reported, her voice tense.

"All right, that's what we want. Take some deep breaths and stay calm. Remember, we want to nab him, not kill him."

Above the rattle and clatter of the bouncing buckboard Fargo heard the steady drumbeat of a rider closing the distance.

"Skye! He has a gun out!"

"His rifle?"

"No. It's a big pistol."

"That's to be expected. Now, stop talking to me or he'll notice."

"Whoa, you hosses!" a man's voice hollered. "Pull 'em in, woman, or I'll irrigate your belly!"

The buckboard slowed, then jerked to a stop. Even hidden under the quilt, Fargo could hear Eb's ragged, excited breathing.

"I finally caught up with you, didn't I, Jezzie? Oh, don't *you* piss icicles, hey? Miss Snooty Bitch herself, actin' like *her* shit don't stink! Not much, I reckon! You filthy whore, I know all about you and that hell-gate twixt your legs."

"Mr. Scofield, I'll thank you to let loose of my team. I wish to drive on!"

Fargo couldn't mistake the double click. He and Marcella were paring the cheese mighty close to the rind. If they had guessed wrong, they were about to find out the hard way.

"You ain't driving nowheres, Jezzie. Now, pull that buckboard off into the trees and light down."

This was the moment Fargo and Marcella had agreed would be their signal: Eb's order that she dismount. Simultaneously, Fargo flung the quilt aside and rose to a crouch, bringing his Colt on bead as Marcella rolled fast to the right to avoid cross fire.

Their timing was perfect and Fargo could easily have drilled a slug through Eb's gunhand. But Eb had deliberately edged his mean claybank in close to the nearside team horse. At the first rustle of the quilt, Eb drove a sharp spur hard into the team horse's neck.

The animal reared in violent protest and jerked the buckboard hard, throwing Fargo on his ass under a face full of clear blue sky. Marcella was thrown across Fargo's legs, partially pinning him down as Eb Scofield started burning powder.

His percussion pistol sparked and fired, its big slug knot-holing the sideboard only inches from Fargo's head.

"*He* won't save you, Jezzie!" Eb taunted. "Watch him die now!"

Again the spark and fire of a big powder load, again a whizzing half-ounce ball tore through the side of the wagon. A splinter of wood pierced Fargo's left cheek.

He had finally worked his legs free and spun up onto his knees. The pistol barked a third time just as he rose, and it felt like a horseshoe had slammed into his head as Fargo again went flat on his back, stunned by a hard crease from Eb's third shot.

A roaring, ringing sound filled his throbbing skull and all of Fargo's limbs went numb. He didn't feel paralyzed so much as boneless—every attempt to move was clumsy and lethargic, as if he were drunk and trying to walk on stilts underwater.

"Skye! *Skye!*"

Fargo knew Marcella's voice was pitched to a frantic warning: Scofield had just peeked cautiously into the buckboard. But her voice sounded faint and far away, and Fargo felt as if he was watching himself in a dream, not facing real danger.

"Skye! *Please*, Skye!"

The peering, unblinking lizard eyes flicked from the stunned and helpless Trailsman to the evil, filthy, beautiful devil bitch, now quailing in the eye-glazed terror of those who know they face eternal nothingness with their next breath or two.

Fargo's ringing skull felt cotton stuffed but some vital instinct within him warned him that the heavy pistol Scofield had just raised into view was not part of a dream.

"Skye, can you hear me? Skye, this is *it*! Do something!"

Fargo had not dropped his Colt when Eb's slug knocked him senseless. Eb drew a bead on Fargo's head, double-clicked the hammer, squeezed the trigger.

Fargo's thoughts were addled, but not his instinct and not his trigger finger. The Colt jumped in his hand, jumped again, a third time and then three more jumps in rapid succession as he emptied the wheel with no clear idea where it was even pointed.

20

"You didn't hit him, but you scared him off!" cried a jubilant Marcella.

Awareness was coming back to Fargo like blood prickling back into a dead limb. By habit he replaced the Colt's empty cylinder with the loaded spare.

His skull throbbed with the mother of all headaches, and it still hurt like hell where a lead ball had burned a line across his scalp.

Fargo cursed without heat. He had been pointedly warned only a few hours ago that Eb Scofield was sneaky and cunning.

"You know that little voice," he said to Marcella, "that nags you? The one that warns you you're being stupid, but you ignore it? I ignored it again."

"Your head," she reported after studying the crease, "is bloody but not bleeding."

"Nothing like a bullet kissing your brainpan," Fargo said, "to make you appreciate your next meal."

He held those alluring green eyes of hers and added, "Or any other pleasure."

"I'm sure Malinda will reap the enjoyment of today's thrills," she barbed. "But I'm glad to see you're getting your . . . spirits back."

Fargo pulled his Henry out from under the quilt.

"I'll stay back here. We best hightail it back to the station. Eb might be laying to pop me over and grab you, or he could fetch the other mad dogs. Depends how much leash Deacon keeps on them."

She clucked to the team. "You say that your plan failed,

and it did—you didn't capture Eb. But, Skye, we're both still alive and we've proved our theories now! Eb behaved exactly as you predicted he would."

Fargo nodded. "The last thing Deacon wants is for you to get hurt or killed—or abducted—while he's in an open contract war with you. This part of it is Eb's private play all the way."

She looked over her shoulder at him. "And evidently Dagobert has played his part in it, too. Are you going to . . . ?"

"Dagobert," Fargo replied, "has been trying to fess up lately. But he gets chicken guts when it's time to stop shoveling that bookish horseshit and get down to cases. I don't think it'll be hard to oil his tongue."

"If he confesses to serious crimes," Marcella fretted, "what do we do?"

"You're the boss, lady, but I take things in the order they matter. What you can do right now is hush down and put on some speed."

Dagobert chafed at his arms to restore blood circulation. He had been tied up for hours and Fargo had just untied the ropes.

He made a pathetic and ludicrous sight as he sat on his bed refusing to meet anyone's eyes. His bandy-legged, rumpled-rag body made Fargo think of a white-haired Humpty Dumpty teetering on the verge of self-ruination.

Fargo, Marcella, Malinda and Stan stood in a semicircle around the bed. Fargo wanted witnesses for this.

"Listen, Dagobert," Fargo said, "I think you know me well enough by now. You know, don't you, that if I decide to wring the truth out of you, I'll succeed?"

"Yes," the Professor said, "I do know that. In fact, a weaker man than you could succeed at breaking me. I'm weak-willed and afraid of pain."

"There you go," Fargo said. "And you being book-learned and all, you must also have figured out that it's just plain hog-stupid not to answer questions."

"My thinking precisely."

"I don't like the prospect of thumping a man your age.

But I've been tortured by several tribes, Dagobert, and I'd be proud to show you a few of their colorful techniques—you know, just in case you decide to be stupid."

"In point of fact, Mr. Fargo, the tribes learned torture from the Spaniards, who—"

Fargo took two quick steps toward the bed and slapped Dagobert—more of a hearty cuff than a slap.

"Knock it off, blowhard. Thanks to spineless assholes like you, there's no time for lectures and mealymouthing. Are you in cahoots with Anslowe Deacon?"

"The wording of your—"

Fargo slapped him again, clearly slaps this time, with a weary, mechanical brutality. "Yes or no?"

"Yes, I reply under duress! But I've never been on Deacon's payroll or been a party to any of his planning."

"Of course you required no money," Marcella said, anger spiking her tone. "Because it's all petty spite, isn't it? Just because you felt cheated—"

Fargo cut her off. "Never mind the you-betrayed-my-trust crap for now."

He looked down at Dagobert. "All right, genius. You figure Tubby gave you the little end of the horn, so you decided to gum up the works for the Scott girls, right?"

"That's a sweeping conclu—"

Fargo slapped him twice this time.

"That's an accurate assessment," Dagobert amended.

"Keep talking," Fargo said, "and keep it simple."

"Deacon approached me in town after Orrin Scott was murdered and the will read. He knew I was . . . discontent. He told me that all he needed was the private financial records of Ozark West."

"Needed for what?"

"He gave me to understand that, armed with that alone, he could ruin Marcella and wrest Ozark West from her."

"You keep the books!" Marcella snapped. "You had to know that's not true."

"Yes, I was suspicious of his claim. But, you see, he also hinted broadly that once he acquired this transfer line, he would then need a competent manager who would be compensated with one-third ownership."

"Look at you," Fargo said, knowing where this was going. "A load of fancy books piled on the back of an ass. All that schoolman talk, yet you were too stupid to see you were being set up for blackmail?"

"In a nutshell, yes, I was too stupid. Once I copied all the financial material and handed it over to Deacon, complete with copious notes in my handwriting, I realized I had trapped myself."

"You knocked Stan out cold," Fargo said, "so that Lem Scofield could fire up the barn, didn't you?"

Dagobert cleared his throat. "Yes."

"A fire that damn near killed a twelve-year-old kid. Were you in on the murder of Tubby Scott?"

"Absolutely not. I swear that by all things holy. I liked Orrin. It was after the reading of Tubby's will that I . . . became disillusioned."

"God, I hate you!" Malinda piped up. "I told Marcella to fire you."

Dagobert ignored her, still talking to Fargo. "I had nothing to do with Jimbo Miller's death, either. I was a cat's paw, not one of the planners."

"Was it you," Fargo said, "who stole that fancy bracelet?"

"No. I was afraid to. Marcella allows no one in her office when she's not there, and I was fearful she'd catch me. Having her complete trust has been important to my goals."

"So you told Eb Scofield about the bracelet?"

Dagobert nodded, smirking as if his tactics had been brilliant.

"Deacon had already suggested him as a go-between. I unlatched one of her windows when Marcella wasn't watching close. Tubby had already shown me the secret drawer. When ill health marooned Truella Brubaker here for several days, I saw an opportunity to please Anslowe Deacon— sufficiently, or so I hoped, to escape his clutches. You see—"

Fargo slapped him. "Never mind your life story. Where's the bracelet?"

Dagobert shook his head. "Fargo, I'm a worm, remember? Deacon and the Scofields don't confide in me."

"So your big idea was to frame Marcella and get Deacon off your back? Instead of shaking him you're still licking his boots. Just last night your information sent Harney Roscoe right to my window to gun me in my sleep."

"I'm surprised that a tough man like you would take such things personally. I never for one moment believed that he could kill you, and I was right."

"I'll give you that one. But you went too far when you brought coffee out to Stan to distract him from Roscoe—you're a self-loving worm, and your 'kind' action betrayed you."

Dagobert looked him directly in the eyes and held the stare for the first time. "That's right, frontier bravo. But I'm not ashamed of any of my actions—only embarrassed that ignorant, ungrammatical lumps of dung were able to out-smart me."

"I *never* liked him!" Malinda exclaimed. "He's an ugly little toad! Hit him, Skye! Smash his little green teeth!"

Dagobert gave her a lazy-lidded look. "Your sister I can't help liking. *You* are a promiscuous—"

"Everybody," Fargo announced, "leave the room except Dagobert and Marcella."

When only the three remained, Fargo grabbed a handful of Dagobert's shirt and twisted it tight in his fist.

"Besides the bracelet," he said in a menacingly quiet voice, "Eb Scofield took something else from that drawer, didn't he? It was never really the bracelet, was it, that had you all giddy with power? It was the other."

Dagobert looked at Marcella, who instantly flushed and turned away.

"Really, my dear," he said, "some souvenirs should be destroyed."

Fargo rocked the Professor's head with a series of fast slaps.

"Bottle it. You're talking to me, not her. You figured this other item would sink Marcella once it got into Deacon's hands. But you've finally figured out, haven't you, that Eb never gave it to Deacon?"

Dagobert scowled. "There's always a weak link. I was definitely stupid there, Fargo. I knew that Eb had sick ideas about women. But I didn't know how else to—"

"You must have some idea," Fargo cut him off, "where Eb keeps it?"

"Absolutely none. It might or might not be with the bracelet."

"He's lying!" Marcella said. "He knows more than he lets on."

"I don't think so," Fargo countered. "The Professor told it straight when he said the rest didn't confide in him. They had no reason to blab the details of their crimes to a weak and foolish man they despise."

He looked at Dagobert again. "If it's necessary you're going to testify at Marcella's trial. And the second you change the facts, Marcella's got a roomful of witnesses to prove you're lying."

"Fine. I don't have the courage to perjure myself. But once I'm under oath I'll have to mention . . . that which may *not* be mentioned."

"Wrong," Fargo said. "Only you, me, Marcella and Eb know about it. And Eb is going to be dead soon. It won't come up at trial, will it?"

Dagobert looked at Marcella. "It certainly *won't* come up if Marcella refuses to prosecute me for my various . . . peccadilloes."

"If you testify honestly and don't volunteer certain facts that aren't part of the trial," Marcella said, "I'll agree to that."

"But you're remaining right here in this room," Fargo told him. "Tied up when there's no one to guard you."

Dagobert looked at Fargo and couldn't control that smirk.

"Fargo, I was never a direct threat to anyone's life, yours included. But those Scofields no longer need orders from Anslowe Deacon. They've figured out that it's you or them."

"A mind like a steel trap," Fargo said sarcastically.

"Oh? Well, to be even more candid, I believe you're about to die."

21

Fargo didn't trust Dagobert Hastings any farther than he could throw him.

He believed the Professor had given more or less truthful answers to his questions. And it seemed logical that Dagobert would keep his courtroom bargain with Marcella—a weakling like him would never survive harsh prison life at hard labor.

But Fargo still didn't trust him. The man was an accountant and bookkeeper, used to figuring percentages and angles. Worse, he was a spiteful man. And if his scheming mind found some way to capitalize on the missing item Marcella so feared, he might still try.

However, any claims about incriminating evidence meant nothing if the evidence couldn't be produced, he informed Cranky Man.

"Which means," Fargo concluded, "I've got to get it before anyone else sees it."

"You already tried," Cranky Man reminded him. "Is this the famous Skye Fargo brain at work—just keep repeating what failed last time?"

It was an hour after sundown and the two men leaned against the back of the house, discussing their situation.

"Yeah, I tried," Fargo said. "But something Eb told Marcella today, when he tried to nab her, has been running through my mind."

Fargo repeated the words: " 'And I got the proof, Jezzie. It might's well be under my feet right now.' "

"Who's Jezzie?"

"He means Jezebel, a white man's name for a good-time

filly. 'Under my feet right now.' That's the part I'm wondering about."

Cranky Man farted with his lips. "Prob'ly just means he buried it someplace."

"And I got a hunch I *might* know where. It's the way he said it—well, it's just a hunch, but I'm playing it. You best turn in, chief. You'll be walking guard for me tonight from midnight to two."

"Damn you, Fargo! Why me? It's no skin off my ass. Get a white man to do it."

"You're the only proven killer in the bunch," Fargo explained. "That's why. Stay close to the house and kill anything that requires killing."

Fargo rode out later as Cranky Man began his own ten-to-midnight watch. It was a warm, windy night with rafts of clouds blowing over and away from the moon in a rapid slide, constantly altering visibility and the shapes of things.

This Ozark country was spooky at night, Fargo told himself. No wonder it gave rise to tales of haunted woods, devil caves and bloodsucking monsters.

He headed due south into the startling landscape of Devil's Den, not liking the fact that he had no idea where any of the four Scofield boys were holed up. Fargo followed the rise and fall of mountain ranges, then began the long descent into the central Devil's Den valley.

Now and then the scream of a puma or the ululating howl of a wolf or wild dog made the Ovaro stutter-step nervously.

"I don't like it either, old campaigner," Fargo soothed him. "But let's keep up the strut. That little voice is telling me where to look, and last time I ignored it I almost got Marcella and me bucked out."

When Fargo reached the old stone-and-log bridge he pulled rein and sat his saddle, listening and looking. The creek, engorged by increasing runoff, rushed by below his feet with the sound of a thousand agitated ghosts rapidly whispering.

The moon was presently obscured by clouds, and Fargo made out little in the darkness ahead except the distant silhouette of the Ozarks like a pod of whales.

Fargo's palms started throbbing. Somehow the air suddenly felt different, textured with imminent danger. A bead of sweat rolled out from under his hatband.

"All right, Eb," he said aloud, "let's see what we got here."

The moment the Ovaro's front hooves hit the bridge, Fargo heard the unmistakable pop of a primer cap. Less than a heartbeat later the pistol erupted as the main charge hurled lead at him.

Fargo's left saddle fender twitched under his leg as the ball tore through it. He had spotted no muzzle flash or the shooter's position. A cautious man would have reined his mount around and retreated to fight another day. Fargo, showing a gambler's nerve, charged into the attack.

He wove the reins into the fingers of his left hand, drew his Colt with his right, and thumped the Ovaro hard with his heels, surging forward as a second shot split the night.

Fargo fired blindly in a semicircle ahead of him, knowing that if he survived this, it would be due to the Ovaro, not his short iron. The stallion was deep-chested for endurance and his hocks were not overly angular—the chief reason horses pulled up lame.

But even the sturdiest horse was not safe running at night, especially across a valley that was like a rocky plateau. Nonetheless Fargo put his chin in the mane and ki-yied the Ovaro to a reckless pace, irons clanging on stone and sending off winking sparks.

Even after he had escaped the ambush, Fargo kept up the dangerous pace. He needed to build a lead, needed to buy time to please that little voice nagging him.

His previous close scout now paid off as Fargo slanted off the trail. There was a narrow but passable ravine close by, slicing between two sandstone bluffs. It would cut a half mile off the distance to Devil's Den Cave. A route all the Scofield boys no doubt knew . . .

It might's well be under my feet right now.

The altar. Fargo had searched the walls around it diligently. But he had paid little attention to the floor of the cave, including in front of the uplift shaped like an altar.

Fargo assumed that it was Eb Scofield who had opened up on him near the bridge. Not only was it the sound of the same cap-and-ball Eb had fired earlier that day, but there had been only one shooter.

So Eb's brothers and cousins weren't with him. Maybe that was their plan, but Fargo had suspected for days now that Eb was on his own secret purifying mission and had gone rogue on his kin. Meaning he was protecting that cave and likely on his way there now.

Fargo let the Ovaro out on his instincts, pushing the stallion through the ravine, among huge fragments of sandstone and limestone, between dangerously deep crevices barely visible in the darkness. The stallion sensed Fargo's urgency and responded flawlessly to every squeeze of Fargo's knees, to the slightest pull of a rein.

Rock debris dotted the cave area and Fargo reined in behind a heap of sandstone fragments. He hobbled the Ovaro and soaked a torch. Leaving the Henry booted, he studied the open ground between him and the entrance to Devil's Den Cave.

Fargo knew he was up against it. From here on out he had to take risks he would rather avoid. Cranky Man was right, and it was no skin off Fargo's ass, either, if Marcella Scott went to jail and Ozark West was devoured by its creditors.

But Fargo was a paid jobber, and he had hired on to face the bullets. His word was his bond, and he was duty-bound to face—even take—those bullets.

He bolted toward the cave entrance and ducked inside without incident. He fired up the torch and made his way farther back into the cave.

The leaping flame of the torch kept distorting objects and shadows, constantly fooling Fargo into thinking someone was leaping out at him. He reached the altar-shaped uplift and knelt in front of it, bringing the torch as low as he could to study the cave floor.

It was a maze of fissures and cracks, and nothing out of the ordinary caught Fargo's eye.

But then his eye picked out one crack that was perfectly straight, and once he had that in view he quickly spotted the other three lines. It was a rectangle slightly smaller than one half of a checkerboard.

Fargo followed the outline until he found a niche, an area

worn in the sandstone as if somebody had been sticking something in it to pry it open. In three seconds he had inserted the point of the Arkansas toothpick into it.

He wedged it in a half inch and pried upward. A lid of sandstone slid loose. Fargo bent to his right and jammed the torch into a crack in the wall to free both hands.

He lifted the lid aside. Someone—Fargo's money was on Eb Scofield—had carved a hidey-hole into the sandstone. And it was neatly filled by a pretty rosewood box.

Fargo pulled the box out and turned the tiny gold clasp securing the top. He was about to lift it when he thought he heard something from the direction of the cave entrance.

Keeping the box in his left hand, Fargo shucked out his Colt and ducked behind the altar formation, watching and listening. He waited a minute but heard nothing except wind moaning when it licked into the cave.

Risks, he reminded himself. You have to take them now.

He set the box on the flat surface of the altar and opened it. The first thing Fargo saw in the torchlight was the brilliant coruscation of diamonds and emeralds—the finest piece of jewelry Fargo had ever seen.

Then he saw what lay under the bracelet, and Fargo forgot everything else in the world, even the danger.

22

"You gorgeous, reckless little fool," Fargo said after a minute of stunned silence.

The clear, perfect camera image had not been reproduced as a tintype but by the new photographic process of printing on paper. It was printed on heavy matte paper and tinted in strategic spots.

Marcella Scott, looking drunk or drugged or both but also quite fetching, sprawled naked on a brown bearskin rug.

Fargo personally considered it a work of erotic art from his point of view as a horny male. The bewitching green eyes, almost always blazing, were lost. But not the perfectly sculpted face and body, the sultry glistening of her lips, the dick-stirring size and shape of her tits, the exciting bush tapering to the tucked-away pleasures no man could stop thinking about for long.

But this same image, however it came into being, had unfairly poisoned a young woman's life and consumed her with fear and shame. Fargo was damn pleased to have seen it, but why a woman would keep it around, especially in a rock-ribbed blue-laws state like Arkansas, baffled him.

He took one last, appreciative look at the photograph while he pocketed the bracelet. Then he passed the photograph through the torch flame, setting it ablaze. Fargo watched it curl up like frying bacon, turning brown and then black.

He now understood Marcella's mysterious behavior. And, in an instant, he turned his full attention to the danger he faced.

The torch was flickering and couldn't last much longer. Fargo pulled it from the crack and started toward the cave entrance.

Carrying the torch made him an easy target, but Fargo

figured his best chance was to get out fast. Without light, in an uneven fracture cave like this one, the abutments and projections made quick movement impossible.

And maybe, after all, a confrontation alone with Eb right here was just what the undertaker ordered.

The torch was burning down and its circle of light rapidly diminishing. Fargo moved as fast as he could, occasionally stumbling.

The sound of a Big Fifty Sharps, inside that natural echo chamber, was deafening and prolonged. The big slug pulverized the sandstone only inches to the left of Fargo's head. He flipped the dying torch behind him and folded to the floor.

Fargo had seen the muzzle flash, but the explosive gunshot broke his focus and it was hard to estimate how far away he'd seen it. He could hear Eb Scofield snicking back the heavy bolt to insert another cartridge.

"You're too late, Eb!" Fargo called out, echoes distorting his location. "I burned it. No more naked devil woman to get you all het up."

"Course you helped her, asshole!" Eb's nasal voice shot back. "She lets you poke her filthy hole."

"Oh, it's not just me," Fargo taunted. "*All* of us at the station top her anytime we get the itch. She even does the Indian."

This was met with absolute silence, but Fargo thought he detected Eb's breathing now, hoarse and ragged as rage boiled within him.

"And you know what, Eb, no shit? Every time she comes she cries out the devil's name."

"Shut your filthy fish-trap!"

"Eb? Oh, you oughta *feel* what that hot little demon can do to your pole. She grinds it, brother, and rattles off backward Latin—that's how devils talk, you know."

"I told you to pipe down!" Eb bellowed. "I don't talk about such filthy shit!"

Fargo continued to tighten Eb's nerve strings. "No, but you sure's hell think about it day and night. Ever since you can remember, you've wanted to know what it's like, hey? What it looks like, what it feels like, what it smells like—maybe even what it tastes like?"

"You're a liar, Fargo, a whoremonger and a hell-born liar!"

Eb's voice was strained to the breaking point. Fargo rolled toward the opposite side of the cave.

"Now me? I've had so many women I'd need a book just to hold all their names. But you, Eb, you stupid, no-dick cracker? I'm going to kill you and you're never going to know the greatest pleasure in the world. A rabbit has more brains than you."

Fargo's strategy produced a snarl of wordless rage before Eb fired the Big Fifty again. The slug flew wide but Fargo got a better fix on the red-orange spear tip of muzzle flash and opened up with his Colt.

He patterned his shots as he rolled into a new position each time he fired, a circle with the spot of the flash at its center. Six o'clock, nine o'clock, high noon, on around the clock until one of his shots drew a sharp grunt in the darkness.

"Gut shot?" Fargo called out hopefully.

"Enjoy yourself, bitch! You're already dead, Fargo!"

By now Fargo had figured out that Eb, in a panic to reach the cave, hadn't wasted time charging and capping his sidearm. Fargo heard the scuttling sounds of retreat.

He didn't bother to pursue. Eb had been much closer to the opening and he knew every inch of the cave. Fargo was perhaps fifty feet from the entrance when he heard hoofbeats fading in escape.

As Fargo emerged, the clouds blew away from the moon, providing just enough silvery light to reveal small blood spatters outside the cave, still wet.

No major arteries or veins hit, a disappointed Fargo concluded. Steady, light bleeding. Eb wasn't gut shot or he'd be on the ground screaming in agony, not escaping on horseback. Still, there was a good chance that even a slight wound would putrefy.

You sold him short before, Fargo reminded himself. And there're three more Scofield boys, two of them smart enough to be even more trouble.

Right now, though, he had to take some news to Marcella Scott, not all of it good.

Light showed under her office door. Fargo knocked and let himself in.

He found Marcella pacing in front of her desk. She glanced at him, then quickly away, her hopes defeated by her fears. She wore a simple white linen wrapper and her eyes were red and swollen from crying.

"I'm glad to see you're still alive," she greeted him. "Cranky Man told me where you went."

"It won't be long now. I wounded Eb Scofield tonight," Fargo said, "and I got this."

He pulled the bracelet from his pocket.

"Skye! I can't believe . . . but how—"

"I'll be keeping it on me for now. It's stolen goods, so I'll ask Sheriff Gillycuddy how to play it. He reads law books."

Hope had sparked in her eyes at sight of the bracelet. But they turned fearful and desperate again.

"And the other?" she asked, holding her breath.

"I burned it up."

"You . . . ?"

She swooned and Fargo reacted just in time to catch her. He guided her to a big armchair.

"Skye, I've been all at sea over it! You *burned* it? Honest to God, it's really gone?"

"Poof. Nothing but ashes."

Great sobs of relief racked her for perhaps two minutes. Then:

"But how do I know you really found it? You could be saying so just to make me feel better."

Fargo grinned. "That's an enticing little heart-shaped birthmark on your bottom."

She flushed instantly. "Yes, you found it."

"You looked drunk or doped up," Fargo said. "Not that it detracted much."

"I was a little of both, I'm afraid, and by my own choice. I was taking an opiate for a horrid toothache, and then I foolishly drank too much champagne."

"You agreed to the photograph?"

"Yes, to my utter remorse. You see, at that time I was involved with the man who took it. He's a portrait photographer in Cleveland."

"Looks like he's a good one."

"Yes, he caters to the wealthy. We . . . we both got too

tipsy, and when Michael suggested an 'art photo,' well, my vanity . . ."

"You have plenty to be vain about, and that photograph *was* a work of art," Fargo said. "It broke my heart to destroy it. But with the way the laws are and all, I'm surprised you kept it."

"It was vanity, mostly. You see, I myself had destroyed the film after Michael made only one copy of me. I liked the way I looked in it and wanted it as a remembrance for my old age. Who knows? Every woman knows that her erotic allure is what draws men most. But I was such a fool to think someone wouldn't eventually see it."

"It'll be on my mind now that I've seen it," Fargo admitted. "It's not something a man can look at and forget. I had already imagined you naked, of course, as any man would. But actually seeing you . . ."

Those bewitching eyes softened in invitation. "Yes. We've both seen the other in very intimate poses, haven't we?"

"You stared at me that night from the doorway," Fargo said, "and liked what you saw."

"It was breathtaking, Skye, seeing you so . . . ready."

"Believe me, I stared at that photograph a long time before I burned it—and I definitely liked what I saw. And I'm *ready* right now."

Fargo unbuckled his gun belt and put it on the desk. "Now that we've both had a good eyeful of each other, and liked what we saw, why don't we get to it?"

"Right here?"

"Sure. Right in that big, comfortable chair you're in."

She smiled. "Well, I *do* owe you one."

"A damn good one," he agreed as he crossed to the office door and turned the lock. "With you on top in my lap."

She stood up and untied the wrapper, shedding it in a puddle at her feet. "Do I live up to the girl in the photograph, Skye?"

"No contest. The real Marcella moves and is starting to breathe heavy."

Fargo studied her with lustful admiration as he dropped his buckskins to his knees, fell into the chair and pulled Marcella, her shapely legs spread wide, onto him. This put her velvet tits in his face, and Fargo, eager to enjoy as much of this beauty as possible, worked her nipples with lips, tongue and teeth.

She adjusted her position and gave a deft wiggle of her hips. They both groaned in overwhelming pleasure as his rock-hard manhood slid into the warm, pliant, willing depths.

Unlike her noisy and dramatic sister, Marcella took her pleasure with quiet intensity. But as the climaxes began to hit with rapid frequency, she plunged up and down on him with an increasingly delirious abandon. Fargo was forced to clasp her taut, rapidly flexing ass to control her as they both gasped into the strong finish.

Minutes later she was the first to speak.

"That was just wonderful, Skye," she said on a long sigh. "I'd say you've had vast experience."

"Practice helps," Fargo agreed diplomatically.

"And you've just brought me such welcome news about the photograph. But I can't forget your first words when you let yourself in: 'It won't be long now.' You're not talking about this station, are you? Nor even our routes?"

Fargo shook his head. "Because Eb is a sick brain and can't be predicted, you need to keep that Greener with you. And try to stay inside. But now *I'm* the red rag to the bulls. Deacon and the Scofields know this is personal now and past mending. Until they kill me nothing else matters. So I have to end it quick on my terms."

23

It was the last meeting ever at the cabin in Blue Holler.

"Where's Eb?" Anslowe Deacon demanded.

"Ain't like we know," Stanton Scofield replied.

Deacon, smelling like the perfume counter at a shop for scrubwomen, stood as close as possible to the door. Lem and Bubba shared the table with Stanton.

"I talked to Harney Roscoe right before Fargo killed him," Deacon said. "According to him, Eb's been a maverick. Disappearing for days at a time in Devil's Den, talking incessantly about Marcella Scott, 'the devil's she-bitch.' He's also been shooting his mouth off about some sort of 'proof' about her that only he knows about."

"That's Cousin Eb for you," Lem said. "It's just like him to give out with a story like that. He uses bluff that way to find things out."

This was a lie and Deacon knew it. But he was in no position to cross these men. His power was based on shaky alliances, and support for him was crumbling in Fayetteville. These hill-trash mercenaries knew too much about him, and only the prospect of plenty of money would keep them quiet and him out of prison.

"Perhaps a good tactic." He backed off, mainly because thanks to Fargo he didn't *have* plenty of money. Good workers, including drivers, had quit, and the sudden shortage of hay and grain, again thanks to Fargo, had cut deeply into his profits.

"We figure Eb to be down in the Den," Stanton volunteered. "That's where we're headed right now."

Jesus Christ, Deacon thought. He had just spotted that ugly black rat poking out of a pocket of Bubba's bib overalls.

The rodent was staring intently in Deacon's direction, nose twitching rapidly as it sampled the air.

"Jimmy likes perfume," Bubba explained, smiling like a proud poppa. "Jimmy likes it, don'tcha? Hanh? Jimmy like?"

Stanton caught Deacon's eyes and winked. "Mite touched," he muttered. "You bring any money?"

"No, but I've set plenty aside," Deacon lied. "You just remember that *all* of us are on the block if Fargo isn't killed."

"Yeah, you worked that out priddy good, squaw man," Lem put in. "You *knew* about Fargo and how he don't let nobody off the hook, happens they try to kill him. But you didn't tell us none a that. Figured to leave us holding the poke. You'd *better* have money set aside, fuckhead, or the Scofield boys will skin you out."

"You gents bragged that you would kill him quickly and I took you at your word. How was I to know you wouldn't come up to scratch? But never mind what can't be changed. This goddamn Fargo measures corn by his own bushel, and unless you employ the same tactics he uses, he's going to win."

Bubba had dozed off. Jimmy edged farther out of Bubba's pocket, rapidly sniffing the perfume-saturated air. His furtive red eyes were luminous with excitement.

"We figured that out already," Stanton said. "But you also knew that none of us reads nor talks much to them. We didn't know how Fargo was writ up in newspapers and such till we heard it in the Hog's Breath."

"And now *we* got to kill him," Lem said. "If that newspaper crowd gets sweet on us for a hanging after we do it, you'll be dropping through a chute with us."

Unnoticed, Jimmy wiggled out of Bubba's pocket and shot down a table leg to the packed-dirt floor.

"Nobody's hanging us," Deacon scoffed, "unless Fargo's body is found. Under Arkansas law murder can't be prosecuted without a body to prove the crime. So just *make sure* it won't be found."

"Going by what I hear in town," Lem said, "Fargo drops out of sight plenty and for long stretches. Nobody would even know to look for him."

"No body, no crime," Deacon repeated. "Just make sure—"

A series of sharp tugs on his wool trousers startled Deacon. He glanced down just in time to watch the huge black rat scuttle onto the ruffled front of his heavily scented shirt. When his mouth dropped open in shocked revulsion, its long pink tail swiped over his lips, the tip popping into his mouth and squirming against his tongue like a man-eating maggot.

The sudden and violent sound when Deacon retched slapped Bubba awake. He opened his eyes just in time to see an ashen-faced and panicked Deacon slap Jimmy from the front of his gal-boy shirt.

"Deacon, you stupid son of a bitch!" Stanton exclaimed.

"No, Bubba!" Lem shouted hoarsely. "Jimmy's all right, see? Just scared, is all."

Bubba threw the table aside so violently that it rocketed into the side wall and broke into three sections. Deacon barely had time to scream before the furious juggernaut was on him.

Bubba clamped one huge bear paw of a hand on Deacon's face, the other on the back of his skull. Emitting a loud grunt at the effort, Bubba jerked the head around with all his considerable force. There was an audible snap when the neck broke.

He dropped the body to the floor of the cabin. Deacon's legs twitched rapidly, much like Jimmy's whiskers, as his last breath rattle-groaned slowly from his lungs.

Lem and Stanton looked at each other for about ten seconds and burst out laughing.

"Get his wallet, Lem," Stanton said. "We'll toss him to old man Brady's hogs when we get back from dousing Fargo's lamp. The squaw man was lying to us about having more money for us, so he ain't no loss nohow."

Lem and Stanton watched Bubba scoop Jimmy up and take him to one of the shakedowns. He rocked the rat back and forth and spoke soothingly to it.

"Hey, Bubba," Stanton said, suddenly inspired. "Deacon tried to kill Jimmy. But you know who put him up to it?"

"Un-unh."

"Skye Fargo, that's who. You 'member him, don'tcha?"

Bubba nodded. "Beard. Killed Cousin Romer."

"'At's right," Lem said. "We're going down to kill Fargo now, Bubba. Me, Eb and Stanton plan to shoot him. But happens we can get you close behind him, you know what to do."

"Skye Fargo," Bubba said, his face twisted in kill frenzy. "Beard. Killed Cousin Romer. Don't like Jimmy."

24

Cranky Man tried to make himself smaller in the saddle.

"Fargo, I know you figure you have to kill this bunch, and maybe you're right. But do you have to make it easy for them to kill us? Why the hell are we riding right out in the open like land surveyors?"

The two men were approaching Mountain Lake at the heart of Devil's Den. It was close to noon and so far no gunshots had broken the still peace of the picturesque Ozark valley.

"We're riding in the open," Fargo replied, "because there's no point in trying to hide from these demented jackals. I've got a good layout of the area, sure. But Dub warned me how this Scofield bunch started hanging around here as kids."

It appeared to be a perfect day for a church picnic. Meadowlarks and wrens flitted, robins chirped, jaybirds scolded angrily. The lake looked like a smooth blue glass mirror reflecting back a vividly detailed image of the trees looming over it.

Perfect unless killers were notched on you. And Fargo assumed they were.

The two men lit down at the east side of the lake to water the horses. Fargo loosened the girth and dropped the bridle.

"We don't want them loggy," he reminded the Choctaw. "Pull your horse back early."

"Fargo," Cranky Man said, too nervous for his usual griping tone, "I hope you know what the hell you're doing. Hell, we might's well be turkeys on a fence."

"Most shots miss the turkey," Fargo reminded him. "Put some stiff in your spine—you've faced worse."

"Damn you, Fargo, that's exactly how you talk when you ain't *got* a plan! You don't, do you?"

"No," Fargo admitted. "But I've got a strategy. That's first cousin to a plan."

Cranky Man touched his magic pebbles and shut up.

An eroded embankment hugged this end of the lake, and Fargo led the Ovaro down into the cold mountain water.

The dreaded sound of the Big Fifty finally came, and water spouted up only inches from the Ovaro's nose. The stallion, spooked but bullet trained, only shied back.

"Looks like they're after the horses!" Fargo called to Cranky Man. "Duck back into the trees pronto!"

The trees were close, but climbing the awkwardly curved embankment forced them to extra exposure as several guns opened up. And now it was clear the two men had been added to the target list as the lead whistled in.

The Big Fifty boom-pounded again, the bullet snapping past Fargo's head close enough for him to feel the tickling wind rip. The remainder of the bullets poured in from hand-guns. The only reason men and horses gained the safety of the trees: they were out of easy short-gun range.

"Save the ammo," Fargo ordered when Cranky Man filled his hand. "I see powder haze out there, but there're too many trees and big rock fragments to hide behind. We'll never get a bead on them from this spot."

"You got a strategy, huh?" Cranky Man carped. "First cousin to a plan, huh? Fargo, you son of a bitch, you're lying! Marcella Scott has got you all pussy-whipped, and you brought me down here to get killed—*that's* your damn strategy!"

"Think into it a little, chucklehead. The Scofield boys have known this place all their lives. They played here and explored as kids, and later they used it for raiding and shaking the law. That tells me they have a secret hideout here that only they know about. A place with shelter from the weather, a place where they feel safe sleeping."

"Like a cave?"

Fargo shook his head. "You hide in caves plenty yourself. But do you prefer them in a shooting fray where an enemy's closing in for the kill?"

"Hell no. Unless you got a secret way out, you're trapped

in a cave. And these caves ain't likely to have secret ways out."

"Yeah. So I don't think we're looking for a cave."

Cranky Man watered the horses from a creek while Fargo served as a roving sentry. The two men hit leather again. Fargo led them toward the area where roughly thirty acres of hillside had collapsed long ago, sliding into the valley and forming the many crevices and caves.

"I thought you said we're not looking for a cave," Cranky Man remarked.

"We're not. I'm interested in the hills just beyond the slide."

"Looks to me like you're more interested in putting us in Eb Scofield's sights."

"I'm sweating that Big Fifty," Fargo admitted. "But we've got us a ray of sunshine, savage. It ain't Eb shooting the Big Fifty—the bullets missed by too much."

"Yeah? Didn't you say you wounded him last night?"

Fargo nodded, watching the bluffs and rock shelters surrounding them.

"That wound must be giving him fits," Fargo said, "if it took a marksman like him out of the fight. Which brings me back to my secret hideout idea—if Eb's not in fighting fettle, where is he?"

"He could be in Devil's Den Cave, maybe—"

"Trouble," Fargo cut in, his voice low and urgent. "*Don't* look or do anything. Just listen. I spotted a rifle barrel up above us on the sandstone bluff coming up. Just keep riding forward."

"Fargo," Cranky Man said in a strained voice just above a whisper, "why'n't we each just break to opposite flanks?"

"They don't know I spotted them, and I never give up the element of surprise. Just follow my lead. Once you empty your wheel, it's hey-diddle-diddle and up the middle—got it?"

Fargo figured they'd be safe until they rounded the shoulder of the bluff and came into full view from above. Just before he did, he speared the Henry from its boot and thumped the Ovaro with his heels.

He shot into view from above with the Henry blazing. For just a moment, before the ambushed ambushers ducked to safety, Fargo glimpsed Stanton, Lem and Bubba Scofield.

He kept the Henry bucking, shell casings clattering everywhere, while Cranky Man emptied his modified revolver and spurted ahead into the cover of rock formations, Fargo dogging him.

"They never got a shot off," Cranky Man boasted.

"I didn't see Eb, either," Fargo said. "But then, that might not be such good news."

The two men stayed on the move throughout the day, usually holding their horses to a walk while Fargo studied each area he had already mapped out in his mind as trouble grids.

He had no interest in chasing at least three and possibly four Scofields all around Devil's Den. Cranky Man had nailed it to the counter: the two of them were turkeys on a fence. And while it was true that most bullets missed at a turkey shoot, it was just as true that the turkeys eventually ended up adding lead to their diets.

The longer Fargo and Cranky Man provided tempting targets, dragging this deal out, the shorter their odds of survival. But find where they holed up, Fargo hoped, and with luck he could force their hand and end it—one way or the other. It was too late for a third way.

Twice more during the day's search they were fired on, nuisance sniping from a distance more than committed attacks. It was for this that Fargo had expended so much lead at the sandstone bluff. He wanted them spooked by his ability to spot them and pour hot fire on them—and thus more inclined to keep their distance.

"See anything?" Cranky Man asked.

Fargo shook his head. The two men had just slowly ridden opposite sides of a long and deep crevice. Most of these long, narrow cracks were useless as hideouts, too restrictive, inaccessible and inescapable. But a few of the wider fissures had staircase ledges carved into them and had to be searched.

"Night's coming on," Cranky Man said, kneading the small of his back. "We need to look for bed ground."

"No, we keep riding," Fargo said. "This thing's come to the fever pitch now. No sleep, we eat in the saddle, and we don't stop longer than it takes for a quick scout or to feed and water the horses."

Fargo handed the Ovaro's reins to Cranky Man and pulled his spyglasses from a saddle pocket. It was that time in the late afternoon when the sunlight was turning brassy and hitting the heart of Devil's Den from a new angle. Experience had taught Fargo that sunlight just past its glory was best for spotting movement by cutting glare and reflection.

He climbed to the top of a rock formation and flopped onto his belly, lying at an angle to avoid reflection from the lenses as he studied the varied terrain around him. He traversed forested mountain slopes, hissing waterfalls, bluffs, ravines, caves and rock formations that could have been fashioned by drunk giants.

He carefully studied the thickets and rock nests along the creek, cave entrances and shadowy pockets among piles of fractured stone. The sun was starting to flare and flatten above the western horizon, but Fargo persisted. If the Scofields did have a hidey-hole, this might be just about the time they'd be returning to it.

He brought the binoculars to bear on the forested mountain slope overlooking the sandstone crevice and cave area. He had searched it earlier, but it still held his interest. The tree cover was especially thick, and it commanded a good view of—

"There," Fargo muttered, focusing finer.

For a full two seconds he had glimpsed the shrewdly angular face of Stanton Scofield. It bobbed into view as he rode through an opening in the tree line halfway up the mountain.

Thirty seconds later Lem rode through the same opening followed shortly by the moon face of Bubba Scofield.

"I just spotted every one of them 'cept Eb," Fargo called down to Cranky Man.

"Headed our way?"

"Nope. They 'pear to be moving up that mountain straight behind you."

"No reason to be over there," Cranky Man said, "with us over here and easy enough to see."

"No reason 'less maybe they're calling it a day and returning to their hideout."

Fargo knew it would be impossible to find their trail after

151

dark unless he fixed a good bearing now. Carefully he moved the binoculars in a straight line to the base of the mountain.

"Wild plum bushes," he told himself, fixing the clump in his mind. The bushes lay in a more or less direct line from the opening through which he'd just spotted the three Scofields. If he started there and managed to hold a straight course in the dark, he might at least be closer to wherever they were holing up.

Fargo climbed back down, his protesting muscles reminding him that weariness was setting in.

"Fargo," Cranky Man said, "we ain't *really* going up that mountain tonight, are we?"

"I am. I told you this thing's got to end."

Fargo counted out $32.50 and offered it to the Choctaw.

"Here's your half of the pay. You been a good pard on this job, Cranky Man. But I can't ask you to take any more risks. In less than an hour you can be back on the rez."

"Hold on to the money," Cranky Man replied. "I've come this far. I might's well stick it out. Malinda is a stupid, mean bitch, but Marcella is all right. But, Fargo, I got a bad feeling about that mountain."

"So have I," Fargo admitted. "But I get that bad feeling a lot and I'm still alive."

25

It was well after dark when they reined in at the plum bushes at the base of the mountain. Both men swung down and led their mounts about ten yards into the thick growth of pine and dogwood trees.

"From here we ride shank's mare," Fargo said. "In close-in forest like that we'll be quieter on foot. We'll leave the horses right here."

"Hobbles or tethers?" Cranky Man said.

"Short tethers so they can graze the pine needles. Don't kick the pin in too deep. We want 'em able to fight or run— there're pumas and wolves in this area. Bears, too."

Fargo used the only system he knew for holding a straight line at night when the stars weren't visible. From the plum bush he picked an object—a lone stunted pine—straight in front of him. He repeated the methodical process as the two men advanced up the dark slope.

Now and then the canopy overhead thinned out and moonlight streamed in. But much of the time the slope was as dark as a coal bin at midnight.

Cranky Man quickly caught on to Fargo's system for holding a straight line.

"Won't work. We're already drifting," he told the Trailsman.

"Pipe down and listen. They could have a guard out."

They moved fitfully higher, the slope steep enough at times that Fargo was forced to brace his legs and lean forward against gravity. Every few minutes he stopped to listen to the night.

Somewhere nearby an owl hooted—or at least Fargo hoped it was an owl and not a good imitation. Wood-burrowing beetles feasted everywhere, their incessant clicking irritating

Fargo like an obnoxious drumming of knuckles. Sometimes all of it was drowned out in a soughing, shivering rustle when the breeze rose to a gust and made thousands of trees swoop and shimmy.

Cranky Man stroked his magic pebbles while Fargo sighted his next bearing: a hummock about twenty feet ahead. Because visibility was often limited, Fargo couldn't always locate a point straight ahead. He had to accept some drifting and hope the left drift canceled out the right drift.

Higher still, Fargo's breathing became uneven as exertion began to tell. At least the trees were thinning out a little and more moonlight was seeping in.

He pushed clear of a bracken of ferns and saw it ahead of him like a Western painting on a calendar: a sleeping horse standing on three legs.

Fargo dropped to his knees, signaling Cranky Man to move up beside him. Fargo counted a total of four horses. They had been left saddled with their reins tied to tree limbs. Normal treatment for an outlaw horse.

"See any of the Scofields?" Cranky Man whispered.

"No, too many trees. Look, you're good at gentling and controlling horses. Go introduce yourself to that bunch while I poke around. Here, hold on to the Henry."

Before either man could move, a voice spoke aloud from so close by that it froze both of them in place.

"Jimmy go poopy too like Daddy, hanh? Jimmy poopy with Daddy? Jimmy's a good boy, hanh?"

So close by that Fargo could have spit on him, Bubba Scofield rose up from behind a clump of hawthorn bushes, buttoning the straps of his bib overalls. Fargo couldn't see the rat in the darkness, but he heard it squeal.

"Yeah, Jimmy scared. Fargo killed Romer, hurt Cousin Eb. Fargo hate Jimmy, hanh? Daddy kill Fargo, Jimmy."

When Bubba had shambled farther away, crushing under-growth beneath his barge-sized feet, Cranky Man leaned in closer to Fargo's ear. "He's *witko*, crazy. I ain't killing that one, Fargo."

Fargo knew that many tribes had a strong taboo against killing crazy men, believing they were bad medicine best left alone.

"Just take care of the horses like I said. I'll be back for you."

"'Jimmy poopy with Daddy'?" Cranky Man repeated, even his whisper heavy with disgust.

Moving as silently as he could, Fargo fell in behind Bubba. The lumbering half-wit aimed toward an erosion cutbank and simply disappeared behind a huge deadfall in front of it.

Fargo waited while the insects droned their incessant rhythm and mosquitoes dealt him misery. After about twenty minutes he drew his Colt and cat-footed closer to the deadfall. He peered cautiously behind it.

It took a minute for Fargo's eyes to assemble it in the dark: a dugout had been fashioned into one side of the cutbank. Flat stones formed a front wall, with a small opening at one end serving as doorway. Small openings had been left in the stone wall as firing ports.

Fur trappers built it, Fargo guessed, not the Scofields. He had spotted its like all over in his wanderings, quickly erected against winter weather or to fight Indians.

And every one Fargo had seen included a second opening for last-ditch escapes.

He circled around the dugout to the back of the bank. After about ten minutes he faintly heard snoring. Guided by his ear, placing each foot carefully, he eventually found a vertical cleft in the bank nearly impossible to see in the dark.

Tucking at the knees beside the opening, he listened. The snoring was louder now.

But what, Fargo wondered, was that familiar putrid stench?

Pus, he decided, not death, at least not yet. It was the stink of an infected, suppurating wound . . .

Something hard suddenly pressed into Fargo's sternum. When he heard the voice he realized, blood carbonating in his veins, the "something" was the muzzle of a Sharps Big Fifty.

"I knew you'd be coming, bitch, and I owe you one," Eb Scofield said, pulling the trigger.

Fargo had learned early in life that few things were as useful, in self-defense, as the simple forearm block. He had used it countless times to stop fists and knives. And now, moving quicker than thought, he used his left forearm to knock the muzzle of the Big Fifty aside even as it spat fire.

The big slug tore through the folds of his shirt, heat licking his ribs from the muzzle flash and starting his shirt on fire. Fargo fired his Colt point-blank, punching a hole in Eb's forehead and dropping him like a sandbag.

Fargo leaped hard to one side just before a scattergun roared from inside the dugout, its load of blue whistlers widening the cleft in the bank. Fargo snapped off six quick rounds into the dugout before rolling to a new spot. He inserted his spare cylinder.

Cranky Man, on the other side of the dugout and unsure where Fargo was, had so far held his fire. The acrid stench of spent gunpowder was thick in the night air.

"Hey, Stanton!" Fargo taunted. "I've killed both your shit-heel brothers! How you like *them* apples, hog-humper?"

"You still got three Scofields to go, Fargo, and you ain't gonna make it!"

"You're just whistling past the graveyard. You're trapped inside that dugout like a corpse in a coffin. Since there ain't going to be no surrendering, you got one choice: come out a-smokin'. So let's waltz."

"You know, Fargo, you're a crusading fool. Anslowe Deacon would have paid you five times what you're making now. All you'll get from Marcella Scott is the crappy end of the stick."

The remark puzzled Fargo. Given Stanton's untenable situation, it was like a man complaining that he hadn't had a chance to eat dinner before his house burned down.

"Marcella Scott ain't your big problem," Fargo reminded him. "*I* am."

"I'm just saying she goes to court tomorrow. And after they sentence her, they'll come after you as her whatchacall-it, accomplice."

This just doesn't ring right, Fargo thought. It didn't fit what was going on. Some kind of game was afoot . . .

"Nice to know you're worried about me," Fargo called back. "Does this mean I'm spoken for?"

"I was you," Stanton said, "I'd get horsed and put Arkansas way the hell behind me. Yeah, boy . . . or has that fine-haired cunny got you all brain-addled, huh?"

Fargo's vague suspicion spiked itself up to a clear warning of danger. There was no point to all this talk about Marcella—unless Stanton only intended to keep Fargo speaking, as if to pinpoint his location.

Lem Scofield, Fargo suddenly thought. He recalled the sheriff's recent warning: *He's a back-shooter, and while the rest are keeping you distracted, he'll sneak up behind you.*

Two openings into the dugout were covered. But now the thought jolted Fargo like a hard punch: what if there was a *third* opening?

Something rustled in the growth right behind him and Fargo cursed himself for a fool.

26

The Trailsman rolled hard and fast to the right as Lem opened up on him with a six-shooter.

Bullets stitched the ground behind him as Lem swung the muzzle to track him. Each time Fargo rolled onto his back he tossed a shot toward the muzzle flash. The two men traded shots until Fargo's fifth bullet evoked a hard grunt in the darkness, followed by the loud impact of a body crashing into the undergrowth.

Fargo searched him out and found Lem rolling on the ground and groaning from a hit to the chest. He drew the hammer back and used his sixth bullet to blow Lem's brains out onto the ground.

"Nice try, Stanton!" Fargo sang out. "Now it's just you and the half-wit!"

There was no answer, but even as he spoke Fargo was thumbing reloads into his Colt.

"Cranky Man!" he shouted. "You still sassy?"

"Yeah, but the rez is sounding better and better."

"There're more than two openings in the dugout! Swing around so you can watch the right side along with the front. I'll cover this side and the other end."

Stanton must have finally realized his goose was cooked to a cinder. Fargo was still moving to a new vantage point when a savage exchange of gunfire erupted at Cranky Man's end.

The guns fell silent and an ominous stillness set in.

Fargo moved toward the position rapidly, advancing from tree to tree and acutely aware that the Choctaw was a piss-poor marksman. Then he spotted Cranky Man standing in a stray shaft of moonlight and lighting his clay pipe. A body lay nearby.

"You mean you actually hit him?" Fargo said in an amazed tone.

"Missed him six times," Cranky Man confirmed.

Then he held his knife out so Fargo could see the blood and gore glistening on the obsidian blade. "It was a lucky toss."

A heartrending sob emerged from the dugout. "Jimmy! Where are you, son? *Jimmy!*"

"Christ," Fargo said, "I'll bet his damn rat got loose in all the confusion."

Choking with fear and grief, Bubba Scofield emerged from behind the deadfall that concealed one side of the dugout.

"Jimmy!" he bellowed, thrashing noisily around. "*Jimmy!*"

"You gotta be shitting me," Cranky Man muttered.

"Bubba!" Fargo barked authoritatively. "Stand still and listen!"

Used to being ordered about, Bubba reacted to Fargo's tone by halting in place.

Fargo heard faint squeals.

"Move real slow to your right," Fargo ordered. "Hear him? Jimmy's close by, but all the gunshots scared him. Move *slow* so you don't frighten him off."

Still quietly sobbing, Bubba did as ordered. A minute later Fargo heard a giant gasp of relief when Bubba bent over to pick up the rodent.

"I won't do it," Cranky Man muttered, "but you're a white man, Fargo. Ain't you gonna pop him over? He's a half-wit but he's still a murderer."

"Half-wit?" Fargo scoffed. "Hell, he's lucky if he's a quarter-wit. Look at him—blubbering over a damn rat. He's not a killer of his own accord—his brother and cousins put him up to it, and now they're all worm fodder."

Bubba heard the two men muttering.

"Fargo don't like Jimmy," he said. "Fargo made Deacon try to kill Jimmy. Bubba killed Deacon. Now Bubba kill Fargo."

Fargo was startled to hear that Anslowe Deacon was dead. But he didn't want to kill Bubba if he could avoid it.

"Bubba," he snapped. "Who helped you find Jimmy?"

The answer was slow in coming. "Fargo helped find Jimmy."

"That's right. I like Jimmy. But if you try to kill me, I'll have to kill you. Then what happens to Jimmy?"

"He . . . Jimmy have no daddy."

"That's right. Your son will be an orphan."

"Fargo, I ain't *even* believing this shit," Cranky Man said in a low tone.

"You don't want Jimmy to be an orphan," Fargo coaxed. "Bubba, get on your horse and ride back to the cabin in Blue Holler. That's your home now—yours and Jimmy's. Nobody will bother you."

"Go home," Bubba said happily, tucking Jimmy in his pocket and trudging toward the horses. "Just me and you, Jimmy. Got our own home now."

"It ain't so crazy at that," Cranky Man said. "Hell, all Bubba had before was a family of rats. At least this one won't push him around and order him to kill."

Five minutes after Bubba rode off, Fargo and Cranky Man could still hear him crooning soothing lullabies to his rat as they descended the mountain.

27

"It was this old codger's one hundred and fifth birthday," Sebastian Kilroy said, "and his friends and neighbors threw a big bash for him. All of a sudden-like he busts out crying.

"'I wish my wife could be here today,' he says, wiping away tears. 'The poor gal died when she was eighty-five. Good Lord, the awful suffering that poor woman went through! But thank God, at least the baby lived.'"

Laughter bubbled around the breakfast table.

"Sebastian," Fargo said, "I'm proud to know you. But I *ain't* gonna miss those cornball jokes of yours."

"Where you headed next, Skye?" Stan McKinney asked.

"Oh, just heading west and trailing the sun," Fargo replied, finishing the last of his biscuits and sausage gravy. "I've got a little money in my pocket, and if I stay away from gambling tables it might stretch for a time."

"Well, thanks to you," Stan said, "I've got a little more money in my pocket, too. Marcella moved me into Dagobert's old job."

"I still say that son of a bitch ought to be rotting in prison," Sebastian opined. "Marcella let him off too easy. She bought him a stagecoach ticket to St. Louis and he left yesterday."

Fargo agreed that Dagobert had gotten off too light. But thankfully Marcella had never been forced to stand trial. After Fargo talked to Sheriff Dub Gillycuddy about what to do with the bracelet in Fargo's possession, Dub came up with an ingenious solution. He rode into Fayetteville with it and told the sheriff he'd found it hidden in a sack of flour in the Scofield cabin.

He had also hauled in the body of Anslowe Deacon. Since there was no one left to prosecute but soft-brain Bubba,

Truella Brubaker had settled for the return of her valuable jewelry.

"Maybe Dagobert cheated the jailer," Stan said, "but Fargo and Cranky Man sure gave that Scofield trash what-for."

"Yeah, but we couldn't've done it," Fargo pointed out, "without all you boys pitching into the game, too. All of you stuck it out and proved you ride for the brand."

Almost a week had passed since the harrowing confrontation down in Devil's Den that finally ended the threat to Ozark West Transfer. Fargo would have left sooner except for Marcella's insistence that he rest up and be waited on hand and foot—a luxury nearly foreign to Fargo's experience. But he was feeling again the tormentin' itch to push over the next ridge.

Marcella and Malinda were both waiting for Fargo out in the wagon yard when he came outside.

"Skye," Marcella said, her eyes shiny with barely restrained tears, "I could never find the language to tell you how grateful I am. Not only for the invaluable service you rendered to me personally, but for what you've done for Ozark West. Uncle Orrin must be smiling right now."

Anslowe Deacon had died intestate with no legal heirs, leaving his Fort Smith Express Company in limbo. His freight business was now being tossed to Ozark West. Marcella had hired two of his drivers and was now negotiating with the city of Fayetteville for the purchase of Deacon's property on Commerce Street at a rock-bottom price.

"Forget about the gratitude," Fargo assured her. "It's been my privilege to know both of you beautiful ladies."

Malinda tugged Fargo aside and rose up on tiptoes to whisper in his ear. "Skye, you could have knocked me over with a feather when I found out Marcella and you did the 'f' word. Tell me God's truth: which one of us is better?"

Fargo did indeed have a favorite, and it was Marcella, but he was not stupid enough to ever answer such questions honestly.

"Muffin," he said, "you tell me—which is better, a delicious peach pie or a delicious apple pie?"

She slugged him on the arm. "You're just being polite. It was me, right?"

"Two delicious pies," Fargo insisted, "and that's all I got to say."

"Brat!"

He kissed both women good-bye and strolled out to the corral. Cranky Man had tacked the Ovaro and now stood waiting for him.

"I saw them two hanging all over you," the Choctaw greeted him. "Fargo, you oughta charge stud fees. You had both them gals hitting high notes until damn near dawn. I spent too much time with my ear pressed to the wall and didn't hardly get no sleep."

Nor had Fargo. Both sisters, knowing he was leaving the next day, had taken turns visiting him all night.

"Marcella tells me you're a wage slave now," Fargo remarked as he checked the cinches and latigos.

"Ahh, she offered me Stan's job as stock tender. I won't stick with it long, but it keeps me off the rez awhile longer."

Cecil came out of the house and offered Fargo a bundle wrapped in cheesecloth. "Malinda said to give you these, Mr. Fargo. It's roast beef sandwiches."

Fargo grinned as he took the bundle from the kid and tousled his red hair. Cecil had taken to wearing a string of magic pebbles exactly like Cranky Man's.

"You going to the blanket, son?" he teased.

"Yessir! I wanna be a Choctaw, not a Texas Ranger."

This remark obviously pleased Cranky Man, but he only said gruffly: "You'll be the first one with a face full of freckles. Now go toss hay into those nets like I told you."

"Bye, Mr. Fargo! Think you'll ever be back?"

"No telling with me," Fargo said. "This country is always rough on me, but it sure is pretty."

The kid scooted off and Fargo said, "I see he's still following you around like a puppy."

"Can you blame the kid?" Cranky Man shot back. "You're just jealous 'cause he decided I'm his hero, not you."

Fargo turned a stirrup and swung up into leather.

"Yeah? Well, it pains me to say it, but you're my hero too, you drunken reprobate. You saved his life *and* mine. I'd be confetti beside Old Granville Pike by now if you hadn't killed that guard that popped up from Deacon's freight wagon. You smell like a jakes and you're a lazy hound, but you are one fierce, bloodthirsty son of a bitch in a scrape."

"No need to slop over, long-tall. I've made worse mistakes than saving you. Besides, you pulled me outta that burning barn and saved my hide in the alley behind Deacon's rooms—I was chanting my death song."

"Well," Fargo said, reining the Ovaro around, "here's hoping you die like a dog in a ditch, you ignorant red savage."

"And here's hoping you die of the drizzling shits, you paleface son of a bitch!"

Fargo was perhaps thirty yards out when Cranky Man bellowed behind him:

"Hey, Fargo!"

He twisted around in the saddle.

"Try to make it back this way sometime! You're a damn good man!"

"Ain't I though?" Fargo yelled back.

Then he gigged the Ovaro up to a trot and headed deeper into the unsurpassed beauty and terrifying danger of the American West, the only home he knew or wanted.

LOOKING FORWARD!
The following is the opening
section of the next novel in the exciting
Trailsman series from Signet:

TRAILSMAN #391
NIGHT TERROR

1861, the Arkansas swamp country—and
the winds of war are in the air.

The thunderstorm threatened to catch Skye Fargo in the open.
He'd hoped to reach the inn he was bound for before it broke,
but the front moved too swiftly. The afternoon sky was dark
with roiling clouds. Shrieking wind bent the trees and the
already humid air was heavy with the promise of the rain to
come.

Fargo needed to seek cover. Arkansas storms could be
gully washers. He wasn't partial to the notion of having his
hat and buckskins soaked clean through. So when he came
to a bend and spied a smaller trail leading off into the woods,
he reined into it, thinking it might take him to a settler's
cabin where he could ask to be put up until the storm passed.
Some home cooking wouldn't hurt, either. He had money in
his poke to pay for a meal.

The wind keened louder and the trees whipped in a frenzy.
In the distance thunder rumbled.

Fargo went around a bend and drew rein in mild surprise.

He'd found a cabin, all right, but it had seen better days. Half the roof had buckled, the front door lay on the ground, and vines hung over the window. Still, it was shelter. Dismounting, he held firm to the reins and led the Ovaro around to the side where an overhang jutted four or five feet. It would protect the stallion from the worst of the rain. Patting the Ovaro's neck, he said, "This will have to do, big fella."

The Ovaro stamped a hoof. It wasn't skittish like some horses were with thunder and lightning, unless the storm was severe.

Fargo tied the reins, shucked his Henry rifle from the saddle scabbard and went around to the front doorway and peered in. There was a dank odor. Warily entering, he kicked the wall to test how sturdy it was. Then, squatting, he faced the doorway and placed the Henry across his lap.

Fargo's stomach growled, reminding him he hadn't eaten all day. There was pemmican in his saddlebags. He should have helped himself to a few pieces, but now it would have to wait.

With a tremendous thunderclap, Nature unleashed her elemental fury. A deluge fell, rain so heavy that Fargo couldn't see three feet, the drops so large that they struck the ground like hail. He heard the Ovaro whinny and glanced through a gap in the wall. The stallion had its head high and its ears pricked, but it wasn't trying to break free.

The downpour continued. Lightning seared the firmament again and again. A particularly vivid bolt seemed to light up the entire sky and lent an eerie glow to the falling rain. The glow faded, but before it did, Fargo could have sworn he saw something silhouetted against the backdrop of the trees, something on two legs, and huge.

Fargo's first thought was that it must be a bear. There weren't any grizzlies in Arkansas, but there were plenty of black bears and some of them grew to considerable size. It might be seeking shelter from the rain, too.

Fargo rose and levered a round into the Henry's chamber. The last thing he wanted was to tangle with a bruin. He waited, but nothing appeared. He was about convinced he must have imagined it when another bolt turned the rain into a shimmering waterfall, and there, barely a long stride from the doorway, stood the great hulking figure he had seen before.

Involuntarily, Fargo's breath caught in his throat. He couldn't make much out. It was a man—that was certain—taller than he was and twice as wide across the shoulders. A man wearing a hooded affair that draped practically to his knees. In the flash from the lightning the man's entire body seemed to blaze with fire. Then the light faded, and Fargo cleared his throat and said, "Who's there?"

There was no answer.

Fargo stepped to the doorway. Cold drops spattered his cheeks and brow as he hollered again, "Who's there? You're welcome to join me." He said that even though part of him sensed an indefinable danger.

Again there was no reply.

Fargo glanced at the Ovaro to be sure it was still there. He faced the doorway as a sound wafted out of the storm, a ululating howl that rose from a low pitch to a high wail. Goose bumps erupted as he realized it must be coming from the throat of the man he had just seen and not from any animal. Taking a step back, he leveled the Henry. He half-expected the apparition to charge out of the downpour but the howl faded and nothing happened.

Fargo stayed standing a long while. Finally he eased down cross-legged and tried to make sense of the giant shape and the eerie cry. He was amid low hills at the edge of bayou country. The locals were a mix of backwoodsmen and denizens of the deep swamps. Poor folks, mostly. They weren't always friendly to strangers but by and large they were hospitable enough.

They weren't known for howling in rainstorms.

Maybe the man was drunk. He recollected that time in Denver when he'd had so much whiskey that when he walked a soiled dove to her boardinghouse, he'd howled at the moon to amuse her.

He listened for another but the rain and the thunder went on unbroken. For over an hour the tempest lashed the earth.

Excerpt from NIGHT TERROR

At last the rain slackened and the thunder faded and the darkness brightened to gray.

Fargo stayed put until no drops fell. Stepping outside, he admired the wet world the storm had left in its wake: the glistening leaves and dripping limbs, the sheen on the grass, the blue pools and here and there a tiny rivulet.

Going to the overhang, Fargo was about to unwrap the Ovaro's reins when he drew up short. Etched in the dirt was a pair of tracks. Footprints, easily the largest he'd ever seen. He placed his own boot next to one and whistled. The other was at least four inches longer and half again as wide. The man was a giant. Fargo was glad he hadn't tried to take the stallion.

Set to climb on, Fargo froze a second time. Squatting, he examined the tracks more carefully. Instead of the rounded edge of a boot or shoe at the front of each, there were five slight indentations. They looked, for all the world, like claw marks. But he was absolutely certain the figure had been a man.

"What the hell?" Fargo said out loud. Scratching his chin, he looked about for more prints.

There were only the two under the overhang. The rest had been obliterated by the storm.

Puzzled, Fargo shoved the Henry into its scabbard, forked leather, and resumed his journey. He had a few miles to go to the inn. It had taken him two days more to reach Arkansas than the army counted on but he'd had a far piece to come.

He reached the main trail and reined to the south, thinking of the meal he would treat himself to. Beefsteak with all the trimmings sounded nice. And a gallon of coffee to wash the food down.

The next moment his empty belly became the least of his concerns.

For there, lying in the middle of the trail, was a human head.